AN AFFAIR OF STATE
A Gourmet Mystery in Eight Courses

AN AFFAIR OF STATE

A Gourmet Mystery in Eight Courses

Robert Benedetti

Santa Monica

Library of Congress Control Number: 2007907786

ISBN 978-0-6151-6529-5

Dedicated to Peter Mills
creator of the Set Gourmet Theatre
(where this story was first told in play form)
and now proud owner of the Chef's Station,
an extraordinary restaurant
in Evanston, Illinois

The Right Honorable Governor Sir Alfred Woodford, OBE
Requests your presence at Governor's House,
Nicosia, Cyprus
Saturday Evening, July 28, 1914

LE MENU

HORS-D'OEUVRES
    Huîtres au Caviar
    Brochettes d'Huîtres Lucifer
    Artichauts a la Grecque
    Duchesses à la Sultane
                                             Dom Perignon 1906

SOUPE
    Consommé Olga
                                              Warre Port 1878

INTERMEZZO
    Figues Fraiches, Frivolities

POISSON
    Fillets of Sole Olga
                             Les Chailloux Pouilly-Fuissé 1912

ENTRÉES
    Sylphides of Ortolans
    Selle d'Agneau de Lait Edouard VII
                              Chateau Rothschild 1892

RELEVÉ
    Filet de Boeuf Talleyrand
                             Chambertin Clos de Beze 1874

SALADE
    Salade Russe

FLAMBÉ
    Bombe Nero
                                  Le Cup de Vin Rouge

DESSERT
    Glace Coucher de Soleil
                                     Fine Champagne

[Note: All the recipes included are from *Le Guide Culinaire* by George Auguste Escoffier, 1903.]

PRELUDE TO THE BANQUET

28 June 1914 – Sarajevo
Memoir of Count Franz von Harrach

As the car quickly reversed, a thin stream of blood spurted from His Highness's mouth onto my right cheek. As I was pulling out my handkerchief to wipe the blood away from his mouth, the duchess cried out to him, "For God's sake! What has happened to you?"

At that she slid off the seat and lay on the floor of the car, with her face between his knees.

I had no idea that she too was hit and thought she had simply fainted with fright. Then I heard His Imperial Highness say, "Sophie, Sophie, don't die. Stay alive for the children!"

At that, I seized the archduke by the collar of his uniform to stop his head dropping forward and asked him if he was in great pain. He answered me quite distinctly, "It is nothing!"

His face began to twist somewhat but he went on repeating, six or seven times, ever more faintly as he gradually lost consciousness, "It's nothing!"

Then came a brief pause followed by a convulsive rattle in his throat, caused by a loss of blood. This ceased on arrival at the governor's residence.

The two unconscious bodies were carried into the building, where death soon took them.

* * *

7 July 1914 – Vienna
Minutes of the Austrian Council on Affairs of State under the Minister for Foreign Affairs, Count Berchtold:

Count Berchtold opens the sitting by remarking that the Ministerial Council has been called to order to advise on the measures to be used in reforming the evil internal political conditions in Bosnia and Herzegovina, as shown by the recent disastrous assassination of the esteemed Archduke Ferdinand at Sarajevo.

In Count Berchtold's opinion, the moment has come for reducing Serbia to permanent inoffensiveness by a demonstration of Austrian and Hungarian power. So decisive a blow could not be dealt without the participation of our allies; consequently, Count Berchtold has approached the German government in secret. The conversations at Berlin have led to a very satisfactory result, inasmuch as Kaiser Wilhelm has most emphatically assured us of Germany's unconditional support in the case of hostilities with Serbia. Italy is also bound to support such action. The support of both Germany and Italy is crucial, as Count Berchtold is clear in his own mind that hostilities with Serbia will entail war with Russia. Nevertheless, the count feels we must be beforehand with our enemies and, by bringing matters to a head with Serbia, must call a halt to the gathering momentum of events; later it will no longer be possible to do so.

Count Berchtold's opening remarks concluded, the question of war was then further argued thoroughly in a long discussion by the Ministerial Council. At the end of this discussion agreement was reached:

(1) That all present wish for the speediest decision which is practicable in the conflict with Serbia, whether by means of war or peace.

(2) That the Ministerial Council agrees with the Hungarian premier that an attack shall only follow after an ultimatum has been addressed to Serbia, and has been refused.

(3) On the other hand, all present, excepting Hungarian Premier Tisza, hold that a purely diplomatic success, even if ending in a startling humiliation for Serbia, would be without value, and that, therefore, the demands to be put to Serbia must be so far-reaching as to pre-suppose a refusal, so that the way would definitely be prepared for military intervention.

* * *

14 July 1914 – Belgrade
Telegram from Alexander, Prince Regent of Serbia, to the Tsar of Russia:

The Austro-Hungarian government yesterday evening handed to the Serbian government a note concerning the *attentat* of Sarajevo. The demands contained in the Austro-Hungarian note are unnecessarily humiliating for Serbia and incompatible with her dignity as an independent state.

Nevertheless, we are ready to accept the Austro-Hungarian conditions which are compatible with the position of an independent state as well as those whose acceptance shall be advised us by your Majesty. But certain of these demands cannot be carried out without changes in our legislation, which require time. We have received a time limit which is too short. We can be attacked after the expiration of the time limit by the Austro-Hungarian Army, which is concentrating on our frontier.

It is impossible for us to defend ourselves, and we supplicate your Majesty to give us your aid as soon as possible. The highly prized good will of your Majesty, which has so often shown itself toward us, makes us hope firmly that this time again our appeal will be heard by his generous Slav heart. In these difficult moments I voice the sentiments of the Serbian people, who supplicate your Majesty to interest himself in the lot of the Kingdom of Serbia.

* * *

24 July 1914 – London
High Tea at Ten Downing Street

With his usual punctuality, Prime Minister Herbert Asquith sat down at the table in his anteroom at Ten Downing Street just as the clock struck four. He settled his trim, athletic frame into his favorite chair and, as was his habit, ran his hand through his close-cropped hair and stroked his copious mustache. His head butler was ready with the first course of a traditional high tea, so-called because it was served at a normal "high" table rather than a low tea table. The accompaniments to afternoon tea had once consisted of simple bread, butter and cakes, but by 1914 it included three substantial courses served in a specific order. First were the savories, which were tiny sandwiches with savory fillings; second were scones served with jam and Devonshire or clotted cream; last were pastries, including cakes, cookies, shortbread and sweets.

There was just one guest with Asquith this afternoon, his foreign minister, Sir Edward Grey, a thin, lanky man who eschewed the facial hair so common among upper-class men. The two of them had just spent an anxious afternoon discussing the events spawned by the assassination at Sarajevo. As the tea was poured and they began to consume the savories, Asquith put down the six-page document detailing the threat to Serbia that Grey had brought him earlier, and which he had just finished reading.

"Damn it all, Edward, is this an ultimatum from Austria or isn't it?"

"Well," drawled Grey, sipping his tea, "it is in the form of an ordinary diplomatic note, but the contents are the most formidable set of demands ever imposed on one state by another. Indeed, it would be fair to say that it was carefully drafted to exclude any possibility of its acceptance. So, yes, it is in effect not only an ultimatum, but more accurately an announcement of an impending attack."

"Is there any chance of heading it off?"

"No." Grey swallowed and took another cucumber sandwich. "The deadline it sets for response expires in just four days. After that, it is hard to say when an attack might occur, but I shouldn't think it would be long in coming."

The Prime Minister couldn't remain seated. He rose and paced the room. "The Archduke Ferdinand was the acknowledged leader of the Austrian war party. His death will not go unavenged. Our best hope is to stop the conflict from spreading beyond the Balkans. How have the other powers reacted?"

"So far, Russia and France are staying well clear of it."

"What about the Italians? Are they not bound to support Austria by the Triple Alliance?"

"Yes, but thank God they have so far resisted the calls to war. After its war with Turkey two years ago, Italy has not been eager to be drawn into renewed conflict in the region. You will remember that just last year, Italy intervened and persuaded Germany to broker a fragile peace between Austria and Serbia. But the killing of the Archduke has shredded the Peace of Bucharest, and at this point the Italians would be hard pressed to stay on the sidelines."

"And the Hungarians?"

"Even though Hungary is Austria's closest ally, the old Iron Duke, Prime Minister Tisza, is urging caution."

"Has responsibility for the assassination been determined?"

"There are a few hopeful developments: all but one member of the Black Hand, the secret society responsible for the assassination, have been captured, and Serbia has renounced the entire organization; and, thankfully, the official Austrian inquest found no proof of direct involvement by the Serbian government."

"Then the case against Serbia is weak?"

"No matter. Berchtold has been waiting for years for an excuse to invade Serbia; it is the first step in what he calls his Plan for the New Austrian Century. The assassination was a godsend for him and for the whole passel of right-wingers in the Austrian army, especially their chief of staff, General Conrad von Hotzendorff. They have seized on the killing of Ferdinand as a call to arms and are portraying it as a full-scale invasion by Serbia."

The butler cleared the uneaten savories and prepared to serve the scones, but Asquith waved him away and moved to the window, where he stood looking out into Downing Street. "The Emperor Franz Josef is a reasonable man; surely he will not follow Berchtold into war without weighing the consequences."

Lord Grey joined Asquith at the window. The rain had started earlier that day and the drizzle persisted; through the streaked window they watched the traffic on Downing Street move slowly by, its sound muffled. A palpable chill invaded the room and the small coal fire in the hearth did little to fend it off.

"The emperor is old," Grey said, "and Berchtold now controls everything he hears. My operatives in Vienna tell me that even the findings of the inquest exonerating Serbia have been kept from him."

"Berchtold must know that an attack on Serbia will force Russia to come to Serbia's aid. Surely Austria isn't strong enough to resist a Russian attack."

"Not by itself, but Germany has promised to back any action Austria might take against Serbia."

"Good Lord," Asquith cried, " when did *that* happen?"

"Three weeks ago, the Sunday after the assassination. We've only just heard about it. It was a hush-hush meeting at the Potsdam Palace in Berlin; there is no hard evidence, but evidently the Kaiser gave Berchtold a virtual blank check, promising full military backing for whatever he might do to Serbia. In return, Berchtold has already partitioned Serbia on paper, promising a healthy portion to Germany, although he publicly denies that Austria has any territorial ambitions in the region."

Asquith led Grey out of the anteroom and back into his office, where he placed both hands on his desk and leaned heavily over them, his high collar pressing at his neck, staring down at the copy of the Austrian ultimatum. "So there is no chance of confining the conflict to the Balkans?"

"None at all," Grey replied. "Russia is pledged to protect Serbia if she is attacked; in turn, France is pledged to assist Russia in case of war with Austria and Germany; and we, in turn, are bound to aid France. It is like a row of dominos ready to fall, each knocking down its neighbor. Once Berchtold invades and Germany joins him, there will be no turning back. It is even possible that America might eventually be involved, being considered a prime enemy by Kaiser Wilhelm, who blames the Americans – specifically the Texans and their Tejano compatriots – for the murder of his brother Maximilian in Mexico. We have intelligence that Germany has even promised to give Mexico territory within the United States if it will launch a distracting war against the Americans."

"Surely Mexico would not risk such a thing?"

"I would have thought it impossible until recently, but the Mexicans arrested several U. S. sailors in Tampico three months ago, and President Wilson has demanded an apology which the Mexicans have so far refused to give."

Asquith sat down heavily. "There appears to be no way to avert a global conflict."

Grey was deep in thought, and after a long silence he turned from the window.

"There may be one slim hope."

"What is it?"

Grey shook his head. "It is so wild a notion that I dare not describe it in detail yet. First I must see how far Russia and France might go to help avert war. It's a long shot, but it's all we have."

* * *

That night Lord Grey embarked on the most important diplomatic mission of his life. It began with a visit to London's notorious Limehouse district. He drew his cape around his neck against the penetrating dampness of the fog. The hansom cab lurched along the cobbled street, past the last of the night revelers and the huddled knots of vagabonds hunched over small coal fires. They glanced up at the government coach with curiosity and hostility, wondering what might bring such a fine conveyance to the impoverished precincts of Limehouse. "Just another toff on his way to an opium den," muttered one.

The cab rattled past a newsboy hawking papers with headlines that shouted "To Hell With Serbia," the paper's response to the king's declaration of seven days of mourning for the fallen Archduke Ferdinand. It was a sentiment that unfortunately reflected the general opinion of the British public. If it came down to a choice between Austria and Serbia, the vast majority of ordinary Brits would choose Austria. Grey knew he was facing a difficult uphill battle if he had to persuade the country to enter a war on the side of Serbia.

Grey had spent a hectic evening working out the details of the desperate plan that had occurred to him that afternoon in the Prime Minister's residence. It was simple in concept: the only way to avert war was to somehow break the Axis of Austria, Germany, and Italy. If Count Berchtold knew that he could not count on the support of both his allies – Germany *and* Italy – he might not attack.

Urgent diplomatic messages had been dispatched. France and Russia, neither of whom was eager for war, had agreed to help find a way to swing Italy over to their side. And now one more crucial step remained to be taken: Italy must be persuaded to go along.

The cab drew up at a dark house. As Grey knocked on the unmarked door, he could see a dim glimmer of candlelight through the shutters of the lower windows. A small flap in the door slid back and a wizened Chinese face peered out at him. "I am expected, under the name Whitestone," Grey said. The Chinese man squinted at him, then slid the flap closed. The door was unbolted and swung open. Stepping into the dim, smoky interior, Grey was immediately struck by an intense, humid heat, and the pungent smell of opium. He had never been in an opium den before, though he knew that many upper-class men had acquired the habit. This particular Limehouse den was known to be discreet, catering as it did to the nobility, and even to some high government officials and foreign dignitaries.

The Chinese man led him back through a rabbit warren of hallways. On either side Grey glimpsed small cubicles in which recumbent figures lay on their sides, long pipes held to their lips by solicitous Chinese women who daubed their foreheads with damp cloths. At the very back of the house, he was led into a comfortable sitting room where a small fire burned in the hearth.

Sitting in one of the arm chairs before the fire was a mountain of a man, who heaved himself up as Grey entered. The Chinese man quietly closed the door as he left, and Grey was alone with Marchese Guglielmo Imperiale, Italian Ambassador to Great Britain. The Marchese gave the impression of being a jolly, empty-headed man, but Grey knew him to be one of the most astute diplomats in Europe.

"Good evening, Your Grace," Imperiale said. "I apologize for this unconventional meeting place, but I assure you it is completely secure and secret."

"I appreciate that, Marchese," Grey answered, "for what I have to propose to you is of the greatest importance and urgency."

Imperiale gestured for him to sit, and together they drew themselves up before the fire. Imperiale lifted a crystal decanter of brandy from a small table between their chairs. The cut crystal projected images of the dancing flames on the dark walls. He poured two healthy snifters full. "Some of Napoleon's favorite," he said, "one of his more desirable legacies."

Grey sipped, then got straight to business. "I'm sure we agree that war in Europe is imminent, and that if at all possible it must be averted." Imperiale nodded. Grey went on, "I think I see a way to accomplish that, if Italy will agree to an arrangement."

Imperiale leaned forward. "Both Premier Salandra and Foreign Minister San Giuliano agree that war is not in anyone's best interest at this time, except perhaps for the Kaiser. But we are bound by our treaty obligations to Germany and Austria."

Grey put down his glass. "Italy would, however, be interested in expanding its territory, specifically in Trieste, Istria, the Trentino, and Dalmatia?"

Imperiale was so surprised by this that he jerked upright in spite of himself. After a moment he took a gulp of brandy and a great breath of air, and settled back in his chair. He stared at Grey intently, then said simply, "What do you propose?"

"My offer is simple and straightforward," Grey said. "If Italy will agree to refrain from giving military support to Austria if it attacks Serbia, England stands ready to pass control of those territories, and perhaps a few others, to Italy. The key, of course, is that Berchtold must be informed of this arrangement at once, before the deadline issued to Serbia has passed and war is declared."

Imperiale understood immediately. "And your hope is that if Berchtold knows he cannot count on Italy, he will refrain from attacking Serbia?"

"That is my hope. His support in Hungary is weak. Prime Minister Tisza is opposed to the war, and Berchtold has resorted to lying to him about his intentions toward Serbia. Even his own Emperor, Franz Josef, is lukewarm to the idea, and if Berchtold did not control all the information coming to the old man, he would probably not sign the order for war. Berchtold is in a very vulnerable position, and this is the moment when we can derail his plans."

Imperiale considered for a time, staring into the flames. "You may just be right," he said at last. "But I am sure that my government would insist that such a treaty between us must remain secret, known only to Berchtold. If word of it were to get out, we would be forced to deny it utterly. Our enemies would use even the hint of such a betrayal to isolate us and drive a wedge between us and our allies."

"I understand entirely," Grey said, "and I can assure you that there is no risk of exposure." He withdrew a roll of parchment from under his cloak. "For our part, I have here our offer in writing, signed by His Majesty. It needs only your signature."

Imperiale reached out for the document, carefully unfolding it with his enormous fingers, and examined it word by word. When he was finished, he looked up at Grey. "But how and where will this be accomplished in so short a time? We have only four days before the deadline."

Grey leaned close and spoke in hushed tones. "The only copy of the treaty will leave tonight for our embassy on the island of Cyprus. There will be a banquet this Saturday, held annually to celebrate payment of our tribute to the Turkish sultan for control of the island. The affair will provide a perfect cover for delivery of the treaty. I will secretly pass word to the Austrians that the treaty will be delivered personally by our governor on Cyprus to an agent of their choice. Berchtold will have no reason to doubt its authenticity."

There was a long silence during which Grey could feel his heart pounding.

"I may live to regret this," Imperiale sighed at last. He spread the document on the table and reached into his coat for his pen. "But I would regret war more."

* * *

26 July 1915 – Vienna
The Imperial Palace

Field Marshal Baron Franz Conrad von Hotzendorff was redfaced, his large white moustache bristling. He paced the length of the spacious office, his saber swinging at his side, the heels of his boots clacking on the marble floor. "Serbia must learn to fear us again. Otherwise, all our territories will be in danger! We are fully mobilized! To lose the element of surprise would be insane! And Russia, which will no doubt try to aid Serbia, is in no way ready for war, as the czar himself has admitted. Every day we delay gives them more time to prepare. We must attack at once!"

"Please, Baron, you and I are in complete agreement. It is only a matter of timing." Austrian Foreign Minister Count Leopold von Berchtold sat stiffly behind his ornate desk, ramrod straight as always, his small mustache impeccably neat, and his nearly bald head shining. Berchtold's steel will and a lifetime of political experience held him well under control, even though this was the most important week of his life, the culmination of years of planning and subterfuge. He continued soothingly to the mercurial field marshal, "We delay only a few days, to satisfy the objections of Hungary."

In truth, it was not only the objections of Hungarian Prime Minister Tisza that had delayed an immediate attack. Their own Emperor Franz Josef, with what Berchtold considered his outmoded sense of honor, had also hesitated, fearing the condemnation of world opinion. But the crisis created by the assassination of the Archduke Ferdinand had given Berchtold an excuse to spirit the emperor away "for his own safety," and now he was isolated under virtual house arrest, with Berchtold as his only contact with the outside world.

"Everything is ready," Berchtold went on. "The emperor has but to sign the invasion order – and when I tell him that Serbia has invaded us, he will not hesitate!"

Von Hotzendorff stopped his pacing as if struck, his eyes widened. "Serbia has invaded? When did this happen?"

Berchtold smiled. "You surprise me, Baron. Serbia will invade the moment I tell the emperor that they have invaded. He will then sign the order for our retaliation. And once the order is signed, it will be academic who invaded first, will it not?"

Von Hotzendorff nodded. "Of course. A brilliant plan, Leopold."

"But first, these vague rumors that Italy's support is weakening must be laid to rest."

"Yes." Von Hotzendorff's hand sought the comforting grip of his saber. "That could present a serious difficulty if Russia were quicker to mobilize than we think."

There was a knock at the door. "Come," Berchtold said.

The door opened and Wolfgang Gruber, the head of the Austrian secret service, entered swiftly and snapped to attention.

"Well," Berchtold asked, "what have you learned?"

Gruber spoke gravely. "There is word, as yet unsubstantiated, that Italy is indeed considering abrogating their treaty obligations to us. We have received a signal that a secret document prepared by the British is to be passed that will confirm Italy's position unequivocally. It is to be delivered by the British governor of Cyprus to one of our agents in two days."

"Damn those Italian swines!" Von Hotzendorff bellowed.

Berchtold held up a restraining hand. "It may be only a rumor." He turned to Gruber. "It is critical that we know with certainty where Italy stands. We must have that document before the ultimatum expires."

Gruber answered in a whisper. "I have sent Streisel to Cyprus, Excellency. He has connections among the natives there and will receive the document. There is to be a banquet at the British governor's mansion this Saturday, and Streisel will make contact then. He will verify the contents of the document, and we will hear from him before the deadline without fail."

With that, Gruber spun on his heel and marched from the room, leaving the deeply concerned count and field marshal behind.

FIRST COURSE: THE APPETIZERS

1. Oysters with Caviar

"Cannot be usual price!" The old fisherman, stinking of sweat and fish, was yelling, his face red, the veins in his neck bulging. It was a well-rehearsed and effective performance. Some of the other fishermen on the dock paused to watch him in admiration. He took a deep breath. "Is holiday, must be more!"

Nicephorous Phocos, called simply Nicky by everyone, wanted to applaud. Instead he put on a stern face and offered a bonus of fifty drachmas. The wily old man, his face sun-darkened and wrinkled, only shook his head. "Double!" he said. Nicky didn't have time to argue. He opened the large wallet marked with the royal coat-of-arms chained to his belt and counted three hundred drachmas into the man's leathery hand, pockmarked with old hook scars. The fisherman smiled, showing the few teeth left in his mouth, and gestured toward the crates of oysters, still dripping, on the dock.

With the help of the fisherman, Nicky hefted the oysters up into the back of the embassy truck. Though it was not yet seven, the heat was beginning to build, and Nicky knew that as he drove away from the coast the heat would rise even faster. During the two hours it would take him to drive to Nicosia (which Nicky privately called by its local name, *Lefkosia*) the oysters would be in grave danger of spoiling. So Nicky gave the old man another fifty drachmas, and together they provisioned the truck with straw bales, in which the oysters were packed with precious ice – for another hundred drachmas! Nicky hoped that Governor Woodford, who had insisted that the *hors-d'oeurves* include several oyster dishes, could justify this outrageous expense on the embassy's accounts. But then, that was not Nicky's problem; his job at present was to get the oysters back safely.

Nicky climbed behind the wheel, flicking a Roman salute at the old man, who cackled. As he pulled away, Nicky couldn't help smiling. The old fox! He knew Nicky had to have the oysters and that these were the last available on this Saint's Day, when the other more devout fishermen of Kyrenia – which the Turks called Girne – refused to sail. Like any of the Greek Cypriots, the old man took special delight in charging the British embassy an exorbitant rate, and though Nicky had to make a show of outrage at the price, in his heart he was glad to see the British money in the hands of his countryman.

Kyrenia, the port closest to the capital city of Nicosia, was a bustling place on most days, but on this sacred feast day it was reflectively quiet. Winding his way up the bumpy, cobbled street that led south, Nicky had to wait for a procession of angelic children, all in white, singing as they followed a statue of Saint Barnabas through the narrow streets toward the Greek Orthodox church that bore his name. For a moment Nicky was transported to that sultry day twenty years past but still fresh in his mind, when he had followed a statue of a different saint in his own town, his family standing proudly alongside the foot-worn street, his mother smiling and waving, his father looming proudly behind her, the smells of the street vendors' offerings making his mouth water in anticipation of the feast that his grandmother and aunts were laying out at the family's farm, the culmination of three days of steady kitchen labor. Would they ever come again, he wondered, such carefree, golden days – either for him or for his country?

Over the children's song, Nicky could hear the church bells ringing. High on the hill above the docks loomed the enormous medieval Kyrenia Castle, while in its shadow the masts of the fishing boats waved slowly as if in homage to the saint, and the brilliant Mediterranean sun sparkled on the green waters of the harbor. Nicky took a deep breath, feeling blessed to have been born on such a glorious island as Cyprus, but simultaneously and equally aggrieved that the island was still, as it had been for centuries, under the yoke of yet another foreign power, the very power from which he made a good living, enough to support his widowed mother and aunts. The old conflict between his dependency on the embassy and his yearning to see this glorious island free sat in his gut like a piece of undigested fish, and gave the sparkle of the blue waters and the slow waving of the masts in the harbor a twinge of melancholy.

Makarios, the imperious chef of the embassy, had insisted that the oysters be as fresh as possible, so Nicky was determined to make record time. The truck bounced violently over the rutted roads and the engine howled in complaint as the truck swung and wove, raising clouds of dust at every hairpin turn as it wound its way up into the foothills of the Kyrenia Mountains, which stretched away to the west, rising to the distant summit of Mount Olimbos, while to the east the brown, parched fields stretched to the sea.

The windscreen was caked with dust and Nicky turned on the wipers, just in time to avoid hitting a shepherd in a wide straw hat who was leading his flock across the road. The roadway was filled by the animals and Nicky slowly forced his way through, honking furiously and nudging more than one of the wooly bundles out of his way. These domestic sheep were much whiter and better-kept than the brown-haired wild sheep, the *moufflon*, who roamed higher in the forests. The shepherd waved his staff and shouted angrily, and his dog barked and snapped at the truck tires.

The road grew rougher as he moved higher toward the pass that led to Nicosia. This northern district of the island was dotted with mines. Some were ancient, abandoned copper mines – the name Cyprus came from *Kipros*, the Greek word for copper – and they dated from the Greek civilization that had thrived here in 1200 B.C. For centuries, the island had been a Greek kingdom, and during that golden age had produced the thousands of precious statues and other antiquities that now were unearthed almost daily in the busy archeological sites intermingled among the mines. Surely, Nicky thought, no other piece of earth has been so poked and prodded, so honeycombed with holes.

And yet it retained its beauty, even against the more recent strip mines built by the British to dig asbestos and the many other minerals with which the island was blessed – or cursed, Nicky thought, since they had made the "Island of Dreams" an attractive target for an endless succession of foreign rulers. Cyprus, he knew, had an unequaled history of foreign domination stretching back over three thousand years to the sad time when those first Greek settlers were supplanted by a succession of invaders, from the ancient Assyrians, Moroccans, Persians, and Romans, to the more recent French, Venetians, and, since 1571, the hated Turks.

And then, forty years ago, the Turks, while keeping possession, had allowed the British to build a naval base at Akrotiri and to administer the island, in return for protecting Turkish lands and payment of a small annual tribute. How like the Turks, Nicky thought, to borrow a navy ready-made and so easily to sacrifice Cyprus as payment. The thought that the British were probably the best of the bad lot of foreign rulers did little to soften his bitterness that in all the thousands of years since those glorious ancient days, Greece had never once ruled the island again.

As the truck crested the pass, a blessedly cool breeze stirred the trees and Nicky allowed himself the luxury of slowing and leaning out the window to breathe deeply and wipe the sweat from his neck and forehead. He looked to the west and was gladdened, as always, by the full glory of Mount Olimbos rising up in the distance. It was named in homage to Olympus, of course, but the name had been changed sufficiently to maintain a respectful deference to the Greek original.

Nicky felt as blessed to live on the flanks of Olimbos as he would to live near the sacred mountain's Grecian namesake. It was in a meadow halfway up the mountain where, as a school boy, he had lost his virginity. It was, in fact, that same meadow to which he had taken Lydia only three days ago. It hadn't been a conscious choice; he had realized the coincidence only after they had arrived. But now he wondered whether his feelings for Lydia didn't unconsciously represent a new passage in his life, as if the loss of his physical virginity ten years ago was now, at age 27, followed by a loss of emotional virginity, a surrender to feelings that were unfamiliar and frightening. He had never experienced a passion as strong except his passion for liberty, and the collision of these two passions filled him with a deep foreboding.

He downshifted and continued over the pass and down into the stifling heat of the valley below.

* * *

Fraulein Burstner gripped the handrails as the ship lurched. Afraid of a repetition of the seasickness from which she had suffered three years ago on this same voyage, she had asked her Aunt Greta, the seasoned world traveler, for advice. Greta had said that she should avoid eating on the day of the voyage, stay on deck, breathe deeply, and fix her eyes on the horizon. She had done all that, but with every roll and pitch of the ship she felt her stomach churn and her mouth fill with bile. Damn! She remembered Greta's joke: There were two stages of seasickness, the first in which you were afraid you were going to die, and the second in which you were afraid you weren't. The joke didn't seem funny now, as she was just passing from the first stage to the second. She began to understand the stories of the seasick sailors who had tied themselves to the mast in order to avoid throwing themselves overboard.

Nevertheless, it was not so much the seasickness itself, though that was terrible enough, but the indignity of it that angered her. Hildegard Burstner, famous correspondent for *Der Geist*, the most widely-read foreign correspondent in Germany, who had covered wars, floods, famines, and just one month ago the assassination of the Archduke Ferdinand, whose dispatches were translated and syndicated all across Europe, was not someone who should be clutching miserably at the rail above a surging sea, retching like a common tourist.

She had managed to travel overland almost the whole way from Germany, except for the brief and placid ferry across the Strait of Bosporus, and had sought out the shortest possible water route to the island. Even so, the ferry from Alanya to Cyprus, a distance of only some ninety kilometers, took five hours, only one of which remained to be suffered. She tried to distract herself from her present misery by thinking about her assignment. She had undertaken more dangerous assignments in the past, of course, but the urgency of the situation and the enormity of the possible consequences made this one very special. Certainly she would have suffered a sea voyage, even one as short as this, for nothing less.

And, of course, for the chance to see Olga again.

* * *

"Harder, harder, Vittorio!"

God, he thought, what does she think I am, a bull? He increased his tempo and the ferocity of his thrusts. He tried to bolster his erection by thinking of his favorite erotic images, flashes of imagined couplings with celebrities, fragments of memories from younger days, bits of pornography.

It was not that she was unattractive; on the contrary, she was by any measure a beautiful woman, even at her age, and had kept her figure surprisingly well. Before they had met, he, like thousands of other men, had fantasized about her. Her reputation as an artist and as a lover was irresistible. Her performance as the coquettish Nina in Stanislavski's earth-shaking production of *The Seagull* had established her as the leading actress of the Moscow Art Theatre. She had swept Europe in triumphant role after triumphant role: Cleopatra, Camille, and the saucy britches roles of the boulevard. Her love life was as famous and intriguing as her acting; she was rumored to have had affair after affair, husband after husband, though never in that order. She had coupled with the most notable avant garde artists of the decade, male and female, and had been wooed by aristocratic playboys across Europe.

When she was in her forties, she had at last found a mature match in Count Tschernisch, famous hunter and explorer, and close friend of Czar Nicolas. When the czar had abdicated, the count and his countess went into splendid exile, traveling the world until his death four years ago in an avalanche on Mont Blanc. She herself had narrowly escaped death in the accident, and after a brief period of mourning had resumed her dissolute ways. Now in her fifties, the roles of her youth were no longer on offer, and she was too proud to accept character parts as madams and mothers. On stage as in life, she was absolutely determined to die an ingénue.

As the offers for leading roles had dwindled, so had the throng of eager young admirers. Eventually, she had been forced to take a series of lesser lovers, although she insisted that they be at least younger than herself and ostentatiously virile. Up-and-coming athletes and popular entertainers became her specialties, and it was a secret joke that agents and managers often pimped for her. Then, just six months ago (six months which felt to Vittorio like an eon), fate had brought him into her life.

It was at a party in Rome. Vittorio was then riding down the backside of the wave of his career as a poet, which had crested four years before when he had published a series of self-consciously offensive poems in a Futurist magazine. He had tended that brief moment of fame like an ailing plant despite vague rumors of plagiarism and no recent sales, and had become a fixture on the Roman party scene as a token artist. He had been excited to meet her; in his college years, he had worshipped her from afar for years and had in his mind a treasure trove of erotic fantasies about her, and so, when she had quite literally fallen into his arms, too drunk to stand, he had eagerly embraced his good fortune and had taken her back to her hotel. Although he was neither young, up-and-coming, nor athletic, she had in her stupor insisted that they make love, and he had easily put aside what miniscule scruples he had about taking advantage of her drunkenness. He had approached the conquest with exultation, but the sad reality of the flesh and blood encounter had washed away the images he carried in his mind. Their lovemaking had been perfunctory and she had quickly lost consciousness. As he gallantly undressed her for bed, he was repulsed by her sagging breasts and wrinkled thighs, not to mention her stentorian snoring.

Still, the scant aura of celebrity that lingered around her kept him by her side in the days that followed, and she had increasingly clung to him. In the weeks since, their lovemaking had become desperate, forced, and frantic. It was as if she thought she might recapture in her increasingly infrequent orgasms her youthful energy; she insisted that they both consume huge numbers of oysters in the vain belief that their lovemaking would be stimulated, and Vittorio was put to the task whenever the opportunity presented itself and he could find no excuse.

So waned was her reputation of late that Vittorio was surprised when she received the invitation to the embassy banquet; it was to be one of the highlights of the international social season. He did not know, and she did not reveal, the secret reason for her invitation. That would become painfully obvious only later.

She had insisted that they come for a two-week sojourn, and he had rented a villa in one of the more rustic (and inexpensive) areas on the north side of the island. Inside its flaking walls they were alone with precious little to distract them, and Vittorio had been pushed to the limits of his endurance. Hoping to reduce her sexual appetite, he had plied her with drugs, which unfortunately had the opposite of the intended result. Now they were coupling twice, even three times a day. He began to fear that she would be the end of him.

"Oh, damn," she said as he faltered.

"I must rest," he gasped, "before the banquet tonight. And you, you must be at your best. I will draw you a bath with those oils you so love. And then a massage."

"All right," the Countess Olga Petrova replied, rolling over, "but first, bring me more oysters, with caviar." Vittorio hauled himself out of the bed, his groin aching, and wrapped himself in his silk robe. He was shuffling toward the kitchen when she called again.

"And of course, more cocaine."

Huîtres au Caviare – Oysters with Caviar

Make some little tartlet crusts by rolling flaky pie dough one-eighth-inch thick, cut into rounds with a fancy scalloped-edged cutter and placed into molds, pricked on the bottom, filled with rice (to preserve the shape) and baked. Discard the rice. When about to serve, place a tablespoon of fine, fresh caviar in each tartlet. Make a hollow in the center of the caviar into which you place a bearded Bluepoint oyster. Season with a little pepper and a drop of fresh lemon juice.

---

* * *

Ernst Streisel, the most accomplished covert agent in the Austrian Secret Police, was a man both revered and feared by his superiors. Revered because he had managed to infiltrate the dreaded Black Hand, spending several years undercover in what was one of the most secretive and dangerous organizations in Europe, and feared because his methods were radical and unpre-

dictable. He was, in fact, so loose a cannon that Gruber, his immediate superior, had several times considered terminating him, fearful that Streisel had "gone native," as the British sometimes put it.

But each time Streisel had proven his value. Gruber had been forced to admit that the man, while ungovernable, was indispensable. When, only two days before the assassination of the Archduke Ferdinand, Streisel had brought word of the plot, Gruber found the idea so outlandish that he had hesitated to act on it. Streisel's suspicions were, after all, based merely on the mailing of a single scrap of a newspaper article announcing the impending visit of Ferdinand to Sarajevo. But Streisel insisted that because of the identity of the sender, and those to whom it was sent, it could only be interpreted as a signal for the plot to come to fruition.

Gruber had finally been persuaded to take Streisel's information to Berchtold. Unlike Gruber, the count was immediately inclined to accept the validity of Streisel's interpretation. But to Gruber's surprise, Berchtold ordered him to do nothing.

It was only after the assassination itself the following day that Gruber realized the brilliance of Berchtold's decision. By refusing to prevent the murder of Ferdinand, Berchtold had given them an excuse for invasion that was far more valuable to the Austrian war party than its much-disliked leader, the Archduke, had ever been.

And now, with the invasion imminent, Gruber gave Streisel the most critical assignment of his career: to rush with all haste to Cyprus, there to receive a document that would be crucial to their plans for war with Serbia. He was to verify the contents and send them his report by the new encrypted radio installed aboard the A65, the fastest patrol boat in the Austrian fleet, now stationed at their secret base at Dubrovnik.

Immediately, Streisel activated his few contacts on Cyprus, and that very night he was underway in the Adriatic at flank speed. Not even the captain was informed of their destination and mission.

2. Oysters Lucifer

The warm summer air and the rocking of the truck on the rutted mountain road almost lulled Nicky into a doze as he descended out of the mountains and into the rolling foothills, carpeted with fruit orchards. Some of the citrus trees were still in bloom, and the scent was so heavy in the air Nicky could taste it.

Lower down, he emerged into the broad plain of Mesaoria, with its endless fields of wheat waving like an ocean in the summer breeze. Nicky had been born near here, on his family's farm well away from the city, and in the distance he could see the spire of his little village church above the wheat. As it always did, the sight filled him with bittersweet memories of those innocent childhood days and the simple pleasures and pains of rural life. How he longed to return to that quiet existence, but life had set him on another, potentially violent path.

Nicky shook himself out of his reverie as he neared Nicosia. The clusters of homes on the outskirts of the city began to displace the farmland, and Nicky was fully alert by the time he guided the truck through the narrow northern gate that pierced the thick, ancient walls around the oldest section of the city, some five kilometers across. Nicky guided the truck expertly through the maze of narrow streets, rumbled over the ancient bridge that spanned the Pedieos River, and entered the broad central plaza before which stood the majestic fourteenth-century Cathedral of Saint Sophia. Horn blaring, the truck wove slowly through the pushcarts and vendors' stalls of the perpetual market that were clustered around the cathedral. On the broad steps of the cathedral, he saw Father Demetrius.

* * *

Father Demetrius saw the embassy truck bouncing into the plaza and recognized Nicky behind the wheel. As the truck passed, he made a diminutive Sign of the Cross in Nicky's direction, a silent benediction. Nicky nodded as their eyes met.

Father Demetrius was not a native Cypriot. He had been born in Athens in a squalid slum on the flanks of the Acropolis, and had taken refuge in the church at an early age. Under the doting patronage of a venerable old priest, he had entered instruction as an acolyte when he was still a teenager. Before he had been ordained, however, he had suffered a crisis of faith that for a time drove him out of the seminary. He had entered the secular world with a vengeance, devouring its pleasures like a starving man at a banquet. After a year of frenetic debauchery, he landed in a paupers' hospital with gonorrhea, cirrhosis of the liver, a severe kidney infection, and the beginnings of consumption. As he hung between life and death, he promised God that if he lived he would renew his faith and devote his life to the work of the church. Nursed back to health by a gruff old nun, he had kept his promise. After his ordination, he was assigned to a remote rural parish on Cyprus, but his extraordinary energy and steely determination had quickly come to the notice of his bishop, and he was soon named to the staff of Saint Sophia's Cathedral. He threw himself completely into the life of his parish and soon, in the way of all converts, became more Cypriot than the Cypriots.

Like the other islanders, Father Demetrius had at first welcomed the British. Emissaries of the British government had publicly espoused the ideal of self-governance for the island. To the vast majority of islanders, self-governance meant *enosis* – *union* – with Greece, and a return to the founding culture of the island. They had hoped that the British would use their influence with the Turks to bring this long-delayed dream to fruition, but gradually it became clear that Britain, like every other foreign oppressor, was interested only in what it could get from the island: asbestos and other minerals, antique works of art for their museums, and most of all a prime military base in the Mediterranean.

As his disappointment with the British betrayal of the promised independence grew, Father Demetrius first joined, then came to lead the *enosis* movement. He was its spiritual mainspring, and to his own surprise, he soon found himself encouraging his otherwise complacent flock to open rebellion. Under the uplifted and indifferent noses of the British authorities, he had secretly built a substantial guerilla force that now numbered some thousand committed members. Nicky, because of his strong position within the embassy, was one of the earliest and most important con-scripts.

And now, the tribute festival had become a rallying point for the movement. This annual two-day festival, beginning with a great banquet and climaxing at noon the following day with the ceremony in which Britain paid its yearly tribute to the Turkish sultan for control of the island, had become the symbolic focus for their simmering rage, an emblem of the way their blessed is-land was used as a mere pawn by others. The festival, when dip-lomats from all over Europe would be assembled on the island, had to be used for some sort of dramatic demonstration that would alert the world to their plight. Father Demetrius prayed for inspiration.

* * *

Nicky shifted into the lowest gear and the truck complained as it labored up the winding road that led to the embassy, a mas-sive stone pile in the manner of English baronial estates, that sat atop the highest hill in the city like a Parthenon on its own Acropolis. At last, in a shower of gravel, it skidded to a stop at the kitchen's loading dock just as the embassy clock was striking ten. Nicky honked the horn urgently. A crew of kitchen helpers rushed out and hauled the crate up the back stairs and into the pandemonium of the kitchen.

Cooks were rushing to prepare the elaborate banquet Gover-nor Woodford had ordered over the objections of Makarios, the beleaguered chef, who even now was yelling orders to his sous-chef, cooks, and helpers. He turned as Nicky came in. "Did you get them?" he asked.

"Yes," Nicky panted, "the only load in port, fresh from the sea."

"Thank God," Makarios said, crossing himself, "another half hour and it would have been too late." He ordered several kitchen boys to get busy shucking the oysters as the poaching pans were readied. "The devil take Woodford and his dinner," Makarios muttered. "Saint Barnabas himself could not have endured it!"

Brochettes d'Huîtres Lucifer – Skewers of Oysters Lucifer

Poach some fine oysters, bearded, in their own liquor; dry them, and dip them into thin mustard. Skewer them, six at a time, on skewers. Dip them in a mixture of well-beaten eggs, salt, pepper, and one teaspoon oil per egg. Next roll them in flour, and then in fine bread crumbs. Fry them at the last moment, and serve them on a napkin.

Makarios turned to check the seasoning of the consommé in the huge stockpot beside the main stove. The burly cook was a distant cousin of Nicky's and had grown up not far from the embassy in one of the poorer sections of the city. Nicky understood that Makarios' motives in joining the *enosis* underground were very different from his own. While Nicky was inspired by a love of the land itself and the desire to reconnect with the island's classical past, Makarios and some others were driven by resentment for the comparative poverty in which most of the native islanders had been kept by their various foreign oppressors despite the vast riches those oppressors extracted from the island and so ostentatiously displayed. When the embassy itself was built by the sweat of Cypriot labor, and filled to overflowing with priceless Cypriot antiquities, the British had by their mindless arrogance insulted and inflamed the natives, whom they considered to be no more threatening than a flock of sheep, fit only to be herded and shorn.

Watching the chef stirring his soup, the muscles of his back rippling under his tunic, Nicky thought that he and Makarios were the two aspects of the *enosis* movement—he cerebral and cautious by nature, Makarios muscular and impulsive. They had tremendous power as long as they worked in consort. But should they fall into disharmony... Nicky shrugged the thought away.

Makarios held out a spoonful of soup to Nicky and asked, "What do you think?"

Nicky blew across the soup to cool it, then sucked it in. "A little more salt."

"Thirteen dishes in eight courses!" Makarios cursed as he sprinkled sea salt into the soup. "The governor says such extravagance is the minimum at state affairs in England and France, where more than twenty courses are often served. I tell him that Cyprus isn't England. He says the embassy is British soil and we must serve as they would in London! It's insane!"

In fact, Nicky himself had argued that a simple dinner of native dishes would be considered quaint and interesting by the foreign guests, but Governor Alfred Woodford, OBE, had insisted on a traditional banquet in the grand manner, which was to say, in the tradition of the great Parisian chef, Escoffier. To make matters worse, Woodford had insisted on selecting certain dishes in honor of various guests, with several courses dedicated to a certain Russian actress with whom, rumor had it, Woodford had once been intimate.

Makarios muttered again, "Insane!"

Nicky patted the sweating chef on the shoulder. "His time here will soon end. Might as well give him what he wants."

* * *

Lydia Seymour sat at the harpsichord and forced herself to run scales over and over. Her fingers had grown stiff with lack of practice; it had been only a week but already it felt like an eternity. The trip had been difficult enough, but the arrangements for her performance at the banquet had been a nightmare. Nevertheless, she was determined to do her best.

Rising from virtual obscurity, Lydia had already established a considerable reputation as a performer, entertaining at a number of high society affairs. In addition to her musical virtuosity, her grace, bearing, and most of all her stunning good looks had made her a favorite on the elite diplomatic party circuit. After a successful appearance at the annual awards banquet of the British Foreign Office – and a rumored tryst with a high-ranking member of the cabinet – she had been selected to entertain here on Cyprus at one of the most important evenings in the government's ambassadorial social calendar, one made even more important by the unstable political situation. Lydia was not only bearing up under the pressure, she seemed to relish it.

Finding a decent harpsichord on this God-forsaken island had been impossible, so one had been hurriedly shipped from the Turkish mainland. The instrument was unfamiliar, and its action hadn't been improved by the sea voyage and the humidity. She had directed Stefano and his men as they had carefully placed the harpsichord on the small raised stage at the far end of the ballroom. It was horribly out of tune and of course there was no one here who could properly tune it. Luckily, Nicky, the Cypriot overseer, had volunteered to help, and together over the past week they had managed to bring it passably into tune.

Nicky had admired her as they had struggled to tune the hundreds of strings. Unlike the other British women he had met, she hadn't hesitated to take the wrench in her own hands, straining against the tension of each string, even wiping sweat from her brow with her forearm like a peasant. "Hard work for such delicate music," she said. They had quickly become friends, and once the arrangements were well in hand, Nicky showed her proudly around his island.

Just yesterday they had driven in the embassy truck part way up Mount Olimbos, then walked to a meadow from which the entire northern coast could be seen. They brought a simple native picnic of cheese, dark bread, cured ham, and wine, and spread it out on a blanket under an ancient cedar tree. As they ate, Lydia was moved by the beauty of the view. "I can see why they call it the Island of Dreams," she said. "It seems timeless. I wouldn't be surprised to see a Greek goddess come over that hill on a chariot."

"It should belong to the Greeks again. Some day it will," Nicky said. It was the first time he had ever spoken to an outsider about his political feelings, having learned to be circumspect because of his sensitive position in the embassy. But there was something about Lydia that inspired trust.

"You consider yourself a Greek, then?" she asked.

"Most of us do. The Turks don't belong here. This is a Greek place and always will be."

She smiled. "Then the British don't belong here either?"

Nicky looked away, unsure of how much more to say. Lydia reached out and touched his hand. "I have no illusions about my country, Nicky. We have built our empire on the broken backs of half the world. They say the sun never sets on the British Empire, but I believe our day is ending and it is already twilight for us."

The sincerity with which she spoke touched Nicky so deeply that he could not help leaning over and kissing her, gently at first, but more passionately as she responded hungrily. They fell back into one another's arms.

Lydia pushed Nicky back a little, but only enough to unbutton her blouse. Nicky watched, scarcely able to breathe. As Lydia pulled her camisole away, Nicky saw a beautiful cameo hanging from a golden chain between her breasts. He lifted it. "This is very old, and beautiful. It looks Greek. Who gave it to you?"

"I don't know," Lydia said. "I've just always had it."

Then she reached out and began unbuttoning Nicky's shirt.

Afterward, they lay spent, feeling the cooling breeze move across their glistening bodies. The thick layer of cedar duff under the blanket was as soft as a featherbed.

Later, as they retrieved their clothing, Nicky said, "I've never met a British woman like you."

Lydia laughed. "No, but then I haven't had your normal British middle-class upbringing either, thank God. I had to learn early on to fend for myself and take what I wanted."

"We Cypriots too must learn to take what we want."

Lydia reached out and touched his cheek with her hand. His last reserve dissolved under her touch. He told her of the dream of *enosis*, and the growing strength of the movement, of the inspiration of Father Demetrius, and how the coming banquet had come to symbolize their frustrations.

Lydia listened intently, with real sympathy. "I know something of these feelings, of being helpless to control my own destiny."

She thought for a time, then said, "Perhaps I can help. I'd like to meet this Father Demetrius."

* * *

Streisel stood beside the captain. The A65 had rounded Crete to the north and now they were speeding south of Karpathos. Somewhere beyond Karpathos, Streisel knew, was the largest of the Dodecanese Islands, Rhodes, where the mighty colossus had once stood at the entry to the harbor. Two years ago, these is-lands had been annexed to Italy. If the Italians were true to their pledge under the Triple Alliance, these islands, like Turkey which lay beyond them, would soon join the glorious Austrian cause. But first this mission must be successfully completed. Cyprus lay dead ahead, still hours away. Streisel removed a sealed envelope from the pocket of his great leather coat. He opened it and handed it to the captain, who held it under the duty light and peered at the coordinates it contained. He looked up at Streisel.

"I know this place," he said. "Kyrenia."

3. Greek Artichokes

Nicky and Lydia hurried down from the mountain and went straight to Saint Sophia's. Nicky parked the embassy truck out of sight behind the huge cathedral, inside the stone yard. The yard was filled with blocks, gargoyles, and unfinished ornaments left from the two-hundred-year construction of the church and now saved for repairs. As they walked through it, Lydia marveled at the workmanship.

"Our island has always been a place of great stonecutting and sculpture," he told her proudly.

Set back in the cathedral's shadow was the ancient rectory, a building of unmistakably Hellenistic origins older than the cathedral itself. Nicky rang the bell, and soon a wizened nun opened the door. She nodded to Nicky and without a word led them into Father Demetrius' study.

It took a few moments for their eyes to adjust to the dusty darkness of the rectory. In the hallway, Lydia noticed a long line of coats of arms hanging from the crown molding overhead. Nicky explained, "Father is writing the history of every family in the parish. All the birth, wedding, and death documents of the past millennium are kept here. It is a life's work."

In the study, a single bare electric bulb cast harsh shadows on the religious art that was tightly packed on the walls from floor to ceiling. Paintings, bas-reliefs, busts, reliquaries, even penitential crosses and lashes were hung everywhere. A large dark armoire stood against one wall, one door ajar, revealing venerable vestments hanging within.

Lydia and Nicky were forced to stand, since the sofa and every chair were piled with stacks of papers and books that spilled off onto the floor as well. "Father is a voracious reader," Nicky said, "but not very well organized."

After a few minutes Father Demetrius came bustling in. Lydia was surprised at his youthfulness, and his modern, even urban demeanor. This was clearly not some rural bumpkin.

"Please excuse my untidiness," he said, "but I don't let Sister Agatha clean here. She straightened up once and it took me weeks to find anything. Here," he said, moving piles of papers from the sofa, "please sit here. May I give you some wine?"

They thankfully accepted glasses of sweet sacramental wine, thick with resin.

Nicky was so excited he could barely contain himself. He explained the reason for their visit, how Lydia was performing at the embassy banquet, how sympathetic she was to their cause, how she had an idea she wished to share with them.

Father Demetrius was at first not entirely pleased that Nicky had revealed so much about the *enosis* movement to this British stranger. But he too was soon won over by Lydia's obvious sincerity and intelligence. "So," he asked her, "what is this idea you have?"

Lydia put down her glass. "You have great passion for your cause, and it is just. But passion will not be enough to drive the British and the Turks from the island. Rebellion is expensive. You will need a great deal of money."

"We have a little," Father Demetrius said.

"But you will need a lot. And you could easily get it."

Nicky and the priest looked at her, wondering what she had in mind.

Seeing the question in their eyes, she said simply, "The sultan's tribute."

The men were nonplussed. "The tribute?" Father Demetrius said. "It is a pittance, a merely symbolic payment."

"Not this year," Lydia said. "This year it is being paid in precious stones from the royal collection: one hundred thousand pounds' worth, to be exact. And despite their enormous value, you can hold them in both hands, easy to hide and transport. They are sitting in the embassy safe even now."

"But why so much?" Nicky asked.

"A deal has been made between Britain and Turkey. I don't know the details."

Nicky was thoughtful. "No wonder Woodford has been so nervous about it." Then to Lydia, "But how do you know this?"

"The payment of the tribute itself is a well-established custom. The unusual nature of this year's payment was inadvertently revealed to me by a boastful minister who had supervised the selection and transportation of the stones themselves." She didn't go on to reveal the delicate circumstances under which this boast had been made.

Father Demetrius was worried. "To steal – would it be justified?"

Lydia pressed him hard. "Of course it would be. The tribute is the ultimate symbol of your oppression. What could be more fitting than that it should be used to establish an independent Cypriot state?"

Father Demetrius was quiet, the moral implications of what Lydia was suggesting playing themselves out in his mind. He was troubled by them, but finally, with logic that would have done a Jesuit proud, he was able to lay them to rest. At last he looked up at her. "But how could such a thing be stolen?"

"There is only one place where the stones could be kept; British embassies are always equipped with a safe."

"Yes," Nicky said, "it is in Woodford's study, behind the royal portraits. But how can we get at them?"

"The banquet gives us the perfect opportunity. You are already planning a demonstration of some sort for the tribute festival, are you not?"

Nicky and Father Demetrius looked at each other.

"Yes," the priest admitted, "we had hoped to find a way to disrupt the payment of the tribute on Sunday."

"But the banquet is a far better target," Lydia said. "A roomful of foreign dignitaries confined in one place. You could take control and deliver your demands, force them to hear your side of the story."

Father Demetrius was intrigued. But he was also concerned. "No one must be harmed in any way. The British soldiers would resist…"

Nicky was excited by Lydia's idea. "We are many, they are few. And I see a way to neutralize the British garrison without bloodshed. No one need be harmed."

"And the safe?" Father Demetrius asked.

Lydia leaned forward. "I need only your demonstration to create a diversion. I can open the safe for you."

The priest was not naïve. He now saw Lydia clearly, even if Nicky didn't, and divined her true motive; yet he did not judge her harshly, thinking only that God had sent this unlikely but welcome answer to his prayers. "And for this, you will keep a share?"

"A fair share." Lydia smiled.

She understood the covert bargain that was passing between them. When she had arrived on the island, she secretly rejoiced when the possibility of a local ally, moreover one strategically placed within the embassy, presented itself. Winning Nicky's co-operation was a major improvement in a plan she had pursued for almost a year now, her plan to infiltrate this particular embassy on this particular night to capture this particular treasure, the crowning achievement of her already illustrious career as a jewel thief. And it was a bonus that she felt a real sympathy for Nicky's cause, and that he was handsome and sweet besides.

"Together," she said, "the jewels can be ours."

Father Demetrius nodded. "And our share of the tribute will be used only to help establish the independence of our people."

"Of course," Lydia said. "I would have it no other way."

* * *

The towering, ornate pendulum clock in the main hallway was chiming half-past seven as Nicky left the sweltering hubbub of the kitchen and climbed the service stairs to the second floor hall, moving past the rows of ancient Cypriot statues, vases, and amphorae that occupied every niche in the embassy and spilled over into the nearby museum the British had established a few years ago. These long marble hallways had a special meaning for him, and he never looked at them without a tightness in his throat. Nicky's mother had been a scullery maid in this embassy, and Nicky's most vivid early memories of her were on her hands and knees, scrubbing and wiping this vast floor. In the forty years since the British had begun to administer the island, working at the embassy had become a tradition in the Phocos family, and Nicky had known for as long as he could remember that he too would go into service here. He had started as a houseboy when he was only twelve, and had risen quickly up the ranks of houseman, under-butler, and butler. Three years ago, when Governor Wood-ford arrived, he had chosen Nicky to be overseer because of his ability to speak fluent English, Greek, and Turkish. Besides his linguistic skill, Nicky had proven to be a natural leader, and now he ran all the day-to-day operations of the embassy and served as liaison with the native population.

Just weeks after he had been made overseer, the priest had approached him with his plan for rebellion. Nicky had been a faithful member of the *enosis* movement for years but had heard only rumors of the burgeoning paramilitary wing of the party. Armed revolt had been in the air for decades, but it seemed out of character with the peaceful and stoic temperament of most is-landers. The idea of Cypriots striking out violently seemed as in-congruous as a fistfight in Plato's Academy. But people, Father Demetrius had said, can only be pushed so far. It was time to act, and fate had put Nicky in a position that was crucial to their plans.

Tonight, things would come to a head at last. All the Greek enclaves fairly hummed with anticipation. As for the small mi-nority of Turkish Cypriots who opposed *enosis* – well, they would soon have to find a new home.

Nicky stepped out onto the balcony over the *porte-cochere*, standing almost hidden behind one of the potted lemon trees, and surveyed the sky. After the recent storms, the gods had finally smiled. It was going to be a fine evening, this 28th of July. The scent of jasmine was heavy in the breeze that blew from the hills toward the sea. The sun was setting behind the sacred peak of Mount Olimbos. The last amber rays made the embassy glow as if on fire.

Below, on the road leading up to the embassy, a line of head-lamps and carriage lights could already be seen snaking its way up the hill, the few civilian guests in horse-drawn carriages, the diplomats and military men in huge touring cars, two small flags fluttering on the front fenders, one the flag of their home country, the other indicating the rank of the occupant. The automobiles queued in the driveway as the first guests began arriving at the front door beneath the *porte-cochere*. So many foreign dignitar-ies! It was an impressive turnout and a compliment to the gover-nor.

Good, Nicky thought, the more the better. He finished his cigarette and snubbed it out against the marble railing, careful to strip the butt and scatter the tobacco, leaving no trace. Governor Woodford was reasonable about most things, but he despised smoking and forbid this simple pleasure anywhere inside the embassy. He had once fired a gardener for sneaking a fag in the greenhouse. It wouldn't do for the governor's loyal overseer to be caught setting a poor example.

* * *

The car bounced as it hit a rut and threw her into him. "My goodness," Shirley cried, "the roads here are worse than back home in Kansas."

Her solicitous new husband John put a restraining arm around her shoulder and with his other hand gripped the strap that hung beside the door. "Hey," he called to the driver, "watch out for the holes!"

The Turkish soldier who was driving had arrived at their hotel a half hour late, and now was hurrying to make up for lost time. He glanced back over his soldier and shrugged, wagging his head apologetically.

"I don't think he speaks English," John said.

Shirley was staring out the window and seemed not to hear him. "Oh, look," she said as they passed a woman carrying a huge basket of long loaves of bread on her back.

"They share the use of a communal oven," John explained.

"What a good idea!" Shirley exclaimed, looking back. "Why don't we do that at home?"

"I don't think the bread companies would be very happy about that."

Shirley giggled, "No, I guess not. They'd call it socialism, I suppose." She laughed again.

John looked at his new wife in wonder. She seemed unflaggingly cheerful. In the few weeks since they had been married, John had never once found her sad, petulant, or cross. Even under the stress of the long trip from New York to Cyprus, with all its difficulties, she never seemed to lose her boundless, wide-eyed delight. In truth, he thought, her incessant cheerfulness had become a little wearing, a little boring even. There were times when he found his attention wandering. It was as if he was living beside a bright, bubbly stream and eventually had begun not to hear its sound. He shook the thought away and reminded himself of his good fortune, the whirlwind romance, the nights of wedded bliss with the most beautiful woman he had ever met.

"Shirley," he said cautiously, "I think it would probably be best if you didn't joke about socialism when we're with other people. Unfortunately, they take it seriously over here, and we don't want to offend anyone."

She nodded and bit her lower lip. It was as close to serious concern as she got. "I have to remember to be more careful. It's just that I get so confused about politics. All these treaties and who's an ally of who, it seems to change every time you turn around."

"Best if you just pay it no mind," John said. He thought to himself, That won't be too hard for you, my dear empty-headed Shirley. But a moment later he was angry with himself for the joke, however private it was.

* * *

Nicky walked back down the service stairs into the comparative cool and quiet of the ballroom just as the clock chimed eight. This largest room in the embassy, with its recently electrified crystal chandeliers and sconces, had been filled with twenty round tables, each seating eight guests. The head table was on a raised dais at the end nearest the stairs leading down from the main hallway.

Nicky approached the headwaiter, Stefano, who watched each of the twenty waiters and twenty busboys like a hawk. Stefano was Makarios' brother, and so another of Nicky's distant cousins. True to the family tradition, Nicky had brought him into the embassy some years ago. Since becoming overseer, Nicky had gradually filled the ranks of the embassy staff with relatives, friends, and other Greek Cypriots, all secretly members of the *enosis* movement. Even the household guard, a mainly ceremonial group under the command of the small garrison of British soldiers stationed in the barracks beyond the gardens, were secretly *enosis* members.

Nicky smiled. Woodford might command the British soldiers, but Nicky commanded the much bigger army of embassy employees and house guards. Blood, after all, was thicker than water, especially Greek blood. This, Nicky thought proudly, was what the British, like all foreigners, failed to understand about his people. All, except for Lydia.

"Everything ready?" Nicky asked.

Stefano nodded. "Everybody knows what to do." The waiters, dressed in traditional Cypriot holiday garb, were ready to circulate through the guests, pouring Dom Perignon 1906 into crystal flutes, and serving tray after tray of the hors-d'oeuvres which Makarios and his minions were feverishly providing. In the spirit of equal representation of Greek interests, Nicky had persuaded Woodford to include among the appetizers his own personal favorite, Greek Artichokes.

Artichauts à la Grecque – Greek Artichokes

Pare very small tender artichokes, cutting the leaves short. Parboil them for eight minutes in lemon water, drain and rinse in cool water, drain again in a sieve. For each twenty artichokes, prepare a liquor of 1 pint water, one-quarter pint olive oil, salt, juice of three lemons, a little fennel and coriander seeds, peppercorns, a sprig of thyme, and a bay leaf. Set to boil, add the parboiled artichokes and cook for twenty minutes. Drain and chill. Serve very cold.

The first guests were arriving. In the foyer, Nicky watched the head butler, a cousin thrice removed, marshal his minions as they greeted the guests, taking the fur stoles from the older women, feather boas from the younger, and top hats and opera capes from the men.

The guests strolled past the grand staircase and into the huge ballroom as a sub-butler passed a discreet card with the names of each party to Gregorio, a swarthy footman stationed at the top of the stairs. As each couple descended the short flight of stairs from the hall into the ballroom, Gregorio announced them. Nicky knew the fondness this class of people had for the sound of their own names, and he had carefully chosen Gregorio for his loud tenor voice and good English pronunciation. Gregorio was one of the few members of the embassy staff who was not related to the Phocos family, but he was a boyhood chum.

Music swirled around the guests, barely audible above the babble of conversation. Lydia was sitting at the harpsichord, stunning in an elegant beaded gown, playing with great intensity, channeling all her energy through her fingers and into the music. From across the room, she threw Nicky a conspiratorial glance. He nodded imperceptibly and felt his blood race.

* * *

In the harbor at Kyrenia, the old fisherman waited until the last glimmer of sunset had subsided and total darkness fell. When the signal had been passed, the old man had immediately readied his boat, checking every detail of the engine and rigging. It wouldn't do to suffer mechanical trouble at such a time, especially not when dealing with Streisel and the ruthless Austrian Secret Police. It wouldn't do at all.

He started his engine and slowly crept out of port, keeping his running lights off, as he had been instructed to do. Because of the late hour and the holiday, his was the only boat on the water. He knew these waters so well after a lifetime of fishing from this port that he was confident he could find his rendezvous point by the moon that would soon rise.

4.   Puff Pastry for the Sultan

Nicky was startled as Shirley's broad Midwestern accent with its pronounced nasal twang cut through the sounds of the crowd. "Gosh, just look at all the marble, and the statues are.... well, they're awfully naked, aren't they?!" Nicky bowed slightly as the maid removed Shirley's wrap. He ran an admiring eye over her. A bit fleshy, she was almost what some would call a Rubenesque beauty. Her long blond hair framed a freshly-scrubbed face, the lips full and fixed in a permanent smile. The overall effect was one of voluptuous vacuity. She arranged her shawl and demurely followed her husband toward the stairs.

Gregorio consulted the card he was handed and called out: "Lieutenant John Benton, Military Attaché of the United States, and Mrs. Benton."

There was a stir. Nicky felt his back stiffen and jaw clench as the tall young man passed, wearing a dazzling white dress uniform. He and Shirley, each smiling with at least thirty-six terribly white teeth, moved down the staircase with athletic ease, nodding to the crowd with that self-confident air, simultaneously unassuming and insufferably indifferent, that only Americans could muster in a Europe teetering on the brink of a cataclysm.

Nicky frowned. With the finely-tuned judgment of someone who had grown up in a long-dominated culture, he distrusted these Americans. He feared the insidious, effortless sweep of American culture that stole not only land and resources, but the very identity of the people it touched. And ever since the Americans had waged war against Spain fifteen years ago—Well, no matter....

The shining couple moved to their place at the head table. The crowd had no sooner quieted than another wave of whispered exclamations swept through it. All eyes returned to the staircase as Gregorio called out, "Her ladyship, the Countess Olga Petrova, escorted by Signore Vittorio Anzilotti."

Gasps and murmurs of appreciation greeted the statuesque woman who seemed to float down the stairs. She was surrounded by a shining aura reflected from her gold lamé gown and the cluster of diamonds riding like sea foam on the waves of her voluptuous bosom. A few steps behind, basking in her reflected glory but keeping a respectful distance, came Vittorio, his black hair shining close against his head, his pencil-thin mustache perfectly groomed, his white silk tuxedo hanging perfectly from his slightly stout frame. Like an ocean liner and its tender, the two of them progressed slowly through the crowd, dispensing demure kisses, waves, smiles, and handshakes.

"She can still make an entrance, I'll give her that," a guttural German voice croaked into Nicky's ear. "But you'd think she could do better than that Italian toad for an escort."

Nicky turned to the source of the voice. His first impression was that of a short man wearing a black tuxedo with a flouncy white dress shirt, the lace front of which spilled out between the satin lapels of the jacket. The black hair was cut in a painfully short pageboy style. But when the eyes, with blue eye shadow and long lashes thick with mascara, met his, he recognized the woman journalist who had covered Woodford's installation as governor three years ago. She had written a painfully scathing account of the British administration, and had outraged Woodford even as she secretly delighted the Greek Cypriots.

"Fraulein Burstner," he said, "how good to see you again."

She peered up at him. "Hello, Nicky. Though I don't think your employer would share your feelings about me. People like the governor are never happy to see journalists."

It was true, Nicky thought. Woodford had resisted the demand of the foreign office that Burstner be invited, but snubbing a newspaper as important as *Der Geist* at this delicate moment in history was unthinkable.

"In any case," Nicky said, "I am delighted that you are here. Perhaps we can manage to give you something better than a diplomatic ritual to write about." Burstner looked at him inquisitively, but Nicky remained impassive.

"Well," she said, looking down at the countess and Vittorio receiving the plaudits of the crowd, "if nothing else, she's always good copy. And so is he, the part-time poet and full-time gigolo."

Gregorio's voice was barely audible under the rumor-mongering following the countess and Vittorio as he announced

"Fraulein Hildegard Burstner of *Der Geist*." Burstner slithered down the stairs, and as she moved into the crowd, people shrank from her as if she gave off a palpable chill. Of all the female guests that evening, she was the only woman who was conspicuously unaccompanied.

The champagne and appetizers were being consumed as quickly as they could be served. The most popular of the many hors-d'oeuvres was a meat-filled puff pastry created by the great Escoffier for the Turkish sultan, and which Makarios had adapted using the little wild hens shot only days before by a rabble of excited guests on one of Woodford's pre-banquet hunting soirées.

Duchesses à la Sultane – Puff Pastry for the Sultan

Stuff little puff pastry choux with a purée of fowl, completed with pistachio butter. Glaze each with aspic-jelly, and sprinkle a little chopped pistachio upon each.

Savoring the exquisite combination of these pastries with the Dom Perignon, the guests wandered from table to table, looking at the place cards that identified where each of them was to sit.

Nicky winced with the memory of the three days he and Woodford had struggled with the seating chart. Keeping potential adversaries apart and assumed allies together made the seating a hopelessly complicated exercise in diplomacy, especially now that the assassination at Sarajevo had sent a shock wave through an already unstable Europe, and rumors of the making and unmaking of secret treaties were rampant. Every change in the seating plan had made others necessary, and several times Woodford had thrown up his hands and started again from scratch.

Lieutenant Benton and his wife Shirley, the only Americans present, were a sort of wild card in the seating chart. Woodford was at a loss to decide on what basis he should place them. America professed neutrality in Europe, but its war with Spain in 1898 was far from forgotten. Austria-Hungary especially was rife with anti-American sentiment, and if Austria had managed to persuade its allies to come to Spain's defense during the Spanish-American War, a world war might have resulted. But since the American was the new attaché, he was deserving of special treatment.

Woodford finally decided to place the Bentons at his own table, beside the guest of honor, Mustafa Ataturk, the sultan's emissary, who was to accept the tribute payment at the ceremony which climaxed the festivities promptly at noon tomorrow.

The seating of the countess and Vittorio presented a special problem. The countess was Russian and would have to be seated with representatives from the Triple Alliance, or at least countries friendly with it. Vittorio, however, was Italian, and the Axis was on the verge of war with the Triple Alliance.

"Leave it to Olga," Woodford had said, "to form an impossible liaison and complicate my life as much as possible."

Then there was the problem of Burstner. Besides her androgynous appearance and extreme disagreeableness, not to mention the grudge Woodford still bore her after her offensive article, she was the only unaccompanied woman, and a German to boot. The few single men available were from countries opposed to Germany. "Perhaps we could make her eat in the kitchen," Woodford said to Nicky, only half joking.

"My lord," Nicky ventured, "there is one other unaccompanied person you are overlooking."

Woodford's brows creased a moment, then he brightened. "Of course, Lydia Seymour! But won't she be playing the whole time?"

"No, she plays only between courses, to help cover the service."

"Well, it's an excellent solution. I nearly forgot to include her at all. Good thing you were thinking of her."

Nicky smiled. It would take a good deal to stop him from thinking about Lydia Seymour.

Woodford was struck by another thought. "Say, this could solve our countess problem. If Olga and this Anzilotti fellow sit with Burstner and Miss Seymour, we can give them two couples with no ties to Europe at all – the Brazilians and the Chinese would be perfect."

So at last, they had settled on this happy solution, and the seating chart was complete. But as Woodford said, "Another assassination and it could all be knocked into a cocked hat between the soup and the fish."

* * *

When the last guest had arrived, Nicky withdrew and walked quickly across the hall to the governor's study. He knocked softly. From inside he heard "Come."

If one had never met Sir Alfred Woodford, OBE, one would know what sort of a man he was by a single glance around his study. It was soaked in British tradition, all wooden paneling, old leather and brocade. Engravings of English country scenes lined the walls. On the shelves were military mementos from the African and Indian campaigns. In a place of honor, on the topmost center shelf, was a splendid ancient Greek vase depicting masked dancers, the jewel of the embassy's extensive collection of Cypriot antiquities.

As stunning as the vase was, however, the most prominent feature of the room was the large oil portrait of King George and Queen Mary that hung above the mantel. A small fire crackled in the fireplace.

Governor Woodford stood in front of a mirror, straightening the rows of decorations on his tuxedo jacket, a red sash splashed across his chest. Around his neck hung the Victoria Cross on its maroon ribbon. Nicky gave a tiny bow of greeting and said, "Everyone is here, your lordship."

Woodford turned from the mirror, lifted the glass of whiskey from his desk, and took a sizeable belt. "Was Anzilotti with the countess again?" he asked with some bitterness.

"Yes."

"And Burstner has arrived?"

"Yes."

Woodford tossed down the rest of the whiskey and muttered, "I really didn't think Burstner would dare show her face here again. The woman has no shame." He pulled on his white gloves. "Is everything in place? The extra guards on the perimeter of the compound?"

"Yes, your lordship, just as you ordered."

"And everything ready for tomorrow's ceremony? Extra security in place?"

"Certainly, sir."

Woodford took a deep breath. "It will be a great relief to have the sultan's tribute safely off the island. I've worried about it ever since it was delivered to us." He glanced at the large painting of the king and queen. "An embassy safe is scarcely an adequate repository for such a treasure, especially at times like these." He and Nicky were the only persons in the embassy who knew that the painting hinged open, and behind it was hidden a stout wall safe. Woodford finished his whiskey, pulled on his white gloves, and said, "Very well, Nicky. Let's greet our guests."

They passed into the hallway and Nicky closed the study door quietly behind them. They walked the short distance to the head of the ballroom stairs. Woodford stepped behind the column and straightened his sash, while Nicky nodded a dismissal to Gregorio, taking from him the heavy staff that was the symbol of the overseer's office. Nicky raised the staff and struck it loudly three times on the marble floor.

By the third blow of the staff, Lydia had stopped playing and the crowd was silent. Nicky called out, "Ladies and Gentlemen, *Mesdames et Messieurs, Signori i Signorini, Damen und Herren*: give audience to his Lordship, Administrative Governor for His Majesty's government on the island of Cyprus, the Right Honorable Sir Alfred Woodford!"

Vigorous applause greeted Woodford as he appeared at the top of the stairs, waving his greeting, gesturing the ovation into silence. "Thank you so much for your kind greeting. On behalf of his Majesty, George the Fifth, and His gracious Queen, Mary, I welcome you all." There was another round of applause and calls of "Hear, hear!"

Woodford raised a gloved hand and pointed to the platform at the other end of the ballroom. "First off, please join me in applauding the talent of a lovely young woman who has been touring the outposts of the empire and bringing her great musical gifts to gatherings such as ours, Miss Lydia Seymour." The crowd turned as Lydia rose from the harpsichord to acknowledge the applause.

Woodford went on. "I know that this is the first visit to this remarkable island for most of you, and we shall do all we can to make it a memorable one."

He paused, and then went on in a more serious tone, "Some of you have expressed concern regarding the unrest caused by the lamentable assassination of the Archduke Ferdinand at Sarajevo one month ago. His Majesty's government sincerely regrets this incident. However, it poses absolutely no danger to any of us here, and every precaution has been taken to ensure your safety." Woodford glanced toward Fraulein Burstner. Pointedly, he went on, "I beg you to disregard warnings of a widespread conflict, a so-called 'world war.' This phrase was invented by some irresponsible journalist, and is mere rumor-mongering."

Burstner, admired in her profession for inventing memorable phrases, including this one, glared up at Woodford and snorted.

"Now," Woodford went on, lightening, "let us return to the happy reason for tonight's festivity. Let me introduce our honored guest, Mustafa Ataturk, representative of the Sultan of Turkey."

The crowd applauded as Woodford gestured toward a large, rotund man with a long, waxed mustache, his head wrapped in a jeweled turban and dressed in an ornate Turkish robe, who waved and smiled broadly, the gold in his teeth flashing in the candlelight.

Woodford went on: "For thirty-six years, the compact between Great Britain and the Sultan of Turkey allowing Britain to maintain its naval base on this island has stood firm. In return for its presence here, Great Britain has paid a modest tribute and has protected the sultan's land from all outside aggression."

Everyone in the room knew it was Russian aggression that the sultan most feared, and many looked toward the countess, who was the only Russian present. The countess smiled blithely.

Woodford continued, "Tomorrow, all that is going to change."

Nicky stiffened. His heart leapt. This was the moment for which he and his compatriots had been waiting.

"Our festivities will conclude tomorrow at noon, the traditional time of the payment by the British government to the Sultan of Turkey of what was in the past a small tribute. However, tomorrow's tribute will be considerably greater. It will be a collection of precious gems from the crown jewels themselves, conservatively estimated to be worth one hundred thousand pounds sterling." Gasps and excited murmurs swept the dining room.

When it had quieted, Woodford dropped his bombshell: "In return for this magnificent tribute and the continued pledge of British protection, I am proud to announce that this lovely island of Cyprus will henceforth be permanently annexed to Great Britain!"

For Nicky, time stood still. The British had shown their real colors at last. There would never be self-rule, never a union with Greece. Now the world would know that the British wanted Cyprus for themselves, just like everyone else over the centuries. Not even the most moderate voices in the *enosis* movement could justify further delay. Nothing could stop them now! Woodford was still talking, his mouth moving, but Nicky could hear nothing but the rapid beating of his own heart. Woodford was gesturing toward the French doors that lined the western side of the ballroom, through which the last glimmer of the sunset could be seen. Then he was looking in Nicky's direction, smiling. Smiling! Now everyone was applauding. Nicky forced his mind back to the present.

Woodford was still talking, waving his gloved hand. Nicky heard only a last phrase, "…the wonderful meal our chef has prepared! *Bon Appetit*!"

This was Nicky's cue to begin the service. He nodded to Lydia. As agreed, she struck up a rousing Vivaldi *Allegro* on the harpsichord. He then nodded to Stefano, who gave another signal, and the kitchen doors flew open. A phalanx of waiters marched out with trays full of the soup, now properly salted, followed by the wine stewards ready to pour the 1878 Warre Port, the last great vintage before the phylloxera disaster.

* * *

The old fisherman peered into the dark. A night fog had risen up and hovered low on the water. He was sure he was approaching the rendezvous point. He cut his engine. The boat settled into the water and rode silently on the swells. Faintly, to starboard, he heard the approaching throb of heavy engines running at near idle. Sounds, the old man knew, were deceptive on the water at night. Something that sounded close might be hundreds of meters away, while in the heavy air some sounds were muted. He readied his dark lantern.

After a few minutes, the engines grew closer. The dark shape of the patrol boat materialized and drew alongside the small fishing craft. The old fisherman opened his dark lantern and flashed the code he had been given: three quick flashes followed by one long one.

By the beam of the light during the last long signal, he could make out the markings on the hull of the patrol boat, the number A65 and a discreet Austrian flag. The deep throb of her diesels slowed and fell silent.

Then there was only the quiet slap of the waves against the hulls of the two boats.

SECOND COURSE: THE SOUP

5. Olga's Broth

Fraulein Burstner glowered at her tablemates, thinking, Look where they put me, a table of outcasts. With the only colored people in the room, the Brazilians and the Chinese. And Olga's gigolo Anzilotti is so dark, he might as well be colored too. And as far away from the head table as possible, practically in the kitchen, stuck up against the stage. I wonder who the empty chair is for?

Burstner's thoughts were interrupted by the countess, who gushed, "What a wonderful soup!" She turned to Burstner. "Don't you think so, Hildy?" Fraulein Hildegard Burstner bridled at the mention of her nickname, as the countess well knew she would; it was a past intimacy that the countess enjoyed violating.

"Yah, it is fine," Burstner muttered, "and of course it is sheer coincidence that it is named for you, eh, Olga?"

The countess pretended to blush and batted her eyes, announcing to the table, "Well, yes, it was invented in my honor by Escoffier himself after the opening of my *Phèdre* in Paris."

Consommé Olga

Grind together one and one-half pounds of very lean beef from an old animal, one fowl's skeleton (roasted if possible) and the white of one egg. Add this to five quarts of cold white consommé and heat to a simmer for one hour. Strain through muslin. Just before serving add a pint of good port wine. Meanwhile, cut into fine julienne a small knob of celery root, the white of four leeks, and the outside scrapings of four small carrots. Stew this julienne in butter, reducing it to a glaze. When about to serve, put a dollop of this julienne in the bottom of each soup dish, add a

---

> *little julienne of salted gherkins, and pour on the consommé with a fine old port.*

The two-hundred-year-old port that had been used in the consommé was also poured at the table. Following the light brittleness of the champagne, it felt warm and velvety. The guests were soon suffused with a pleasant inner glow.

The countess raised her glass to propose a toast. "Let us drink to peace. It is such a beautiful evening that I am sure not even the Germans will be stupid enough to spoil it by declaring var."

Burstner drew herself up. "It is not we Germans who threaten war, Olga, but the Austrians."

"What's the difference? You are practically the same, no? So, everybody, I say drink up and enjoy!" She raised her glass of port and tossed it down like a thirsty sailor, then laughed her trill of a laugh, which an infatuated swain had once likened to fairy bells echoing through the Elysian Fields.

It set Burstner's teeth on edge, that laugh, and she remembered the nights when she could hear Olga in the room above, rehearsing it until it had become almost natural. What play was it she was rehearsing then? Burstner wondered. Aloud she said, "Wasn't it one of those Marivaux farces?"

The countess darkened. "What's that, my dear?"

"That laugh, wasn't it for *The Game of Love and Chance*?"

The countess laughed again, almost convincingly.

By this time, everyone in the room had been served, and Lydia finished the *Allegro*. There was a polite round of applause as she bowed. She came down from the stage and approached the one empty chair at the table. Burstner thought, Of course, they put me with the musician!

Vittorio rose and held Lydia's chair, saying, "You play so wonderfully, *bella signorina*, as if the spirit of Vivaldi lived in you."

Lydia dropped her eyes demurely. "That is high praise coming from a famous Italian poet."

Burstner nearly choked on a spoonful of consommé, thinking, Look at her, the brazen little bitch! Does she think she is fooling anyone with this absurd come-on?

Lydia lifted a spoonful of soup, and Burstner watched her closely as she sipped it. Lydia looked up and met Burstner's gaze. "You must be the journalist. Fraulein Burstner, isn't it?"

"Yah," Burstner answered without looking away.

The countess said, "Hildy is a great patron of the arts, Miss Seymour. Like many who have no special talent of their own."

Before Burstner could reply, Woodford rose from his place at the head table and tapped a fork against his wineglass. The room quieted and Woodford spoke. "Ladies and gentlemen.... I'm sure you have noticed the extensive collection of priceless Cypriot antiquities housed here in the embassy. They were collected over the years by my predecessors. Our collection, however, is not the world's largest; alas, that distinction belonging to the Metropolitan Museum of New York, thanks to the patronage of Mr. Andrew Carnegie. But with our annexation of the island will come renewed archeological exploration and controls, so we hope that our collection will soon equal, and even surpass, Mr. Carnegie's!"

A smattering of polite applause distracted everyone but Burstner from noticing that the Cypriot waiters, to a man, stiffened at this promise of renewed pillaging of the island's sacred sites. For as long as any of them could remember, the island had been systematically plundered of its antiquarian riches, sometimes in the name of archeology, sometimes in the name of art, but always to enrich foreign collections.

Woodford went on. "Speaking of Mr. Carnegie, I am proud to say that we have word from him tonight. It is with great pleasure that I introduce Lieutenant John Benton, our new American attaché, making his first visit to our island." Woodford gestured toward John with a flourish. "Lieutenant Benton!"

Benton rose to a round of polite applause. His white fulldress naval uniform glowed in the light from the many crystal chandeliers and sconces. He smiled and said, "Thank you, Governor Woodford, and thank you, ladies and gentlemen. I won't keep you from your dinners, folks. As Governor Woodford said, I bring you the personal greetings of Mr. Andrew Carnegie, who as you know has a special affection for this island and its art. From Mr. Carnegie and all the American people, again, I bring you good wishes and the hope that the recent troubles in the Balkans remain mere clouds on the distant horizon of your beautiful island."

There was another round of polite applause. Burstner let out a snort that made several people look in her direction. The countess glared and through clenched teeth hissed, "Do give the poor dears a chance, Hildy."

John went on. "On a happier note, I want to take this opportunity to introduce my new wife. Shirley, say hello to everyone."

Hesitantly Shirley Benton rose, looking uncomfortable in her ball gown, and curtsied. Burstner thought to herself, *Mein Got*, look at those udders.

In a nasal twang that cut through the ballroom like a knife, Shirley said, "Hello, everyone." She started to sit, then felt the need to say more. "It's a really nice place you have here, lots of marble."

As Shirley sat down, Burstner thought, She has the brains of a cow as well.

Benton, seemingly unfazed by his wife's gaucherie, went on. "We've only been married a few weeks, folks, and my assignment here is a wonderful honeymoon for us! Shirley has already been busy shopping in the native markets; we may have to build a new wing on our house back home to house *her* collection."

During the laughter that followed, Burstner noticed dark glances exchanged between several of the waiters. She wondered what could move these normally docile natives to risk displaying so much displeasure.

Woodford quieted the applause, then concluded, "And now, ladies and gentlemen, we will enjoy what our chef calls an *intermezzo*, a chance to clear your palates with some of our island's natural bounty, and, I expect, a chance for some of you, especially the ladies, to freshen up."

* * *

As the hallway clock was chiming half-past nine, Makarios left his *sous-chef* in charge and went into the meat locker. He picked through the hanging sides of meat and various *salumi*, and found what looked like a large wrapped *proscuito*. He carried it with care out onto the loading dock.

Right on schedule, a produce truck pulled in from the driveway. Makarios guided the driver of the truck as he backed up to the kitchen door. When the truck was in position, he stepped to the cab and whispered to the driver, "Hurry up, Nicky is everywhere tonight."

The driver clambered down and they moved to the back of the truck. The driver asked, "Why not just cut him in? There's plenty to go around."

"My cousin is a man of principle," Makarios chuckled. "He and that priest of his would take a dim view of our little sideline. It's best if we do not burden their consciences with it."

When they were sure no one else was in sight, they pulled aside the tarpaulin from the back of the truck and quickly lifted down a large container marked "PERISHABLE." Makarios jimmied loose the top and lifted out bags of lettuce, onions and peppers, and bundles of parsley, spices, and other foodstuffs, which they piled on the loading dock. When the container was empty, he reached in and felt around for a moment. "Ah, here it is," he said and pulled up a loose board at the bottom, revealing a hidden compartment. From it, he lifted out a package wrapped in burlap.

He laid the package on the stairs, and by the light streaming from the kitchen door, he carefully unwrapped it. Under the burlap was a layer of waterproof oiled canvas. He cut the stitching that held it closed. Inside were a number of white paper packets. He opened one, inserted his finger, then placed the finger in his mouth.

"Yes, it is fine," he said, and closed the packet. "Now for the return journey."

Makarios lifted the bundle he had brought out from the meat locker and laid it carefully inside the hidden compartment. "Third century," he said, "a beautiful figure." He packed straw around the precious antiquity. "Be careful with it," he told the driver. "Art is probably the only thing worth more by weight than cocaine."

They returned the container to the back of the truck. The driver asked, "What about the money for Vittorio's share?"

Makarios shrugged. "He promises it later tonight."

"That is not how we do business."

"Look, it's a madhouse here. This banquet. It's just a few hours more. Come back later with another load. We have a lot of customers tonight, all these visitors."

"It'll take me a little time."

"Well, don't take too long."

Nicky came to the kitchen door and looked out into the darkness. "Makarios? Are you out there?"

Makarios hurriedly tucked the bundle of cocaine under his chef's tunic and waved the man away.

The truck pulled away as Makarios came up the steps carrying a crate of lettuce to cover the bulge in his tunic. Nicky was nervous. "What are you doing out there at a time like this?"

"A fresh load of greens for the salad," he said, pushing past Nicky. "I better get the boys to bring the rest of it in."

"Has the word reached everyone?"

"Yes, yes. Everyone is gathering as planned. Now let me get back to my fish!"

* * *

On most holiday nights, the bulk of Nicosia's population would be in one of two places. Most people would be kneeling in the cathedral, running rosary beads through their fingers, intoning responses to the priest's invocations. Meanwhile, a smaller but not insignificant group, mostly men, would be packed into the three taverns near the central plaza. On this July night, however, Saint Sophia's contained only women, children, and a few infirm old men too ill to fight. And more significantly, the taverns were empty and dark.

That morning, Father Demetrius had sent out the call. It had gone from home to home, church to church, tavern to tavern. Men and older boys had prepared themselves. From closets, barns, and sheds they had collected shotguns, pistols, scythes, axes, anything that would serve as a weapon. Then, singly or in small groups of two or three so as not to attract attention, they had walked past the cathedral steps, where Father Demetrius had stood sprinkling them with holy water to bless their undertaking. They had continued soundlessly, resolutely, toward the thick forests that carpeted the foothills behind the embassy.

* * *

The patrol boat dropped anchor slowly, to avoid a splash. Streisel swung his full-length black leather coat out behind him and pulled his slouch hat down hard on his head. He climbed down the embarkation net that had been deployed over the side. With only a silent nod at the old fisherman, he settled into the stern of the boat.

The old man started his engine and pulled away from the patrol boat, which sat silently at anchor. He turned back and aimed the small craft toward the harbor. His passenger sat perfectly still and uttered not a word during the trip to the harbor, silently contemplating the distant lights of the town as they grew nearer, and the enormity of the task that awaited him.

THE INTERMEZZO

6. Fresh Figs and Frivolities

As soon as Woodford announced the intermission, the busboys began to clear the soup dishes and port glasses, and the waiters carried in huge platters of fresh figs and the elegant little *frivolités* often served as *hors-d'oeurves*, but here intended to cleanse the palate before the delicate fish course. The intermission was also designed, of course, to provide an opportunity for the ladies to visit the powder room.

The countess rose. "Well, you must excuse me, please." Anzilotti popped up and pulled back her chair. He bowed as she swept away, followed by the eyes of the other diners. The countess' exit was taken as a signal by many of the other women and there was a general stir as they rose, thankful for the break. On the stage above them, Lydia began playing one of Schubert's love songs.

Anzilotti smiled at the rest of the table. "You know the ladies, always the powdering of the nose, eh?"

Burstner got up abruptly and said, "I too must be excused. The line in the women's room will be very long."

When she had gone, Vittorio leaned toward the remaining guests. With a malicious smirk, he tapped the side of his nose and whispered, "I assure you the powder does not all go *on* the nose, eh?" He chuckled. The Brazilians and Chinese stared at him uncomprehendingly.

Tartelettes et Barquettes

This special pastry is suitable for tartlets and barquettes (boat type crusts) which differ only in their shape. Sift one pound of flour on to a mixing board; make a hole in the center, into which put a pinch of salt, ½ pound of cold, melted butter, one egg, the yolks of two, and a few drops of water. Mix the whole into a paste, handling it as little as possible; roll it into a ball and

> *let it chill for two hours. Roll it out to a thickness of one-eighth inch, and stamp it into small fancy shapes, round or scalloped for tartlets, oval for barquettes. Prick the bottoms lest they should blister, Place them in baking molds and fill with rice or flour. Bake in a moderate oven; remove the rice or flour (the sole object of which was to preserve their shape.) Garnish them in various ways. For example, coat the bottoms with shrimp, crayfish, or lobster mousse, and upon this lay a very white poached oyster, or a slice of hard-boiled egg cut with a scalloped fancy-cutter. In the center of the yolk put a little lobster coral, and coat the whole with clear aspic. Any cook, with a little taste and inventiveness, can easily make an endless variety of combinations.*

* * *

Olga was trembling by the time she reached the women's toilet. She had rushed to be the first inside and chose the rearmost of the three marble-lined private stalls, each with its own ornate louvered door for complete privacy. Sitting on the commode, she hurriedly withdrew an ornate silver snuffbox from her bag and opened it. She was shaking so violently that she almost spilled some of the precious white powder.

She reached for the delicate gold chain around her neck, grasped it, and pulled it up out of her bodice. From it dangled a tiny silver spoon. Trying not to tremble, she lifted a spoonful of the white powder from the snuffbox to her right nostril. Holding her left nostril closed with her free hand, she drew in a mighty breath. The cocaine struck the inside of her nostrils with a fiery jolt, and try as she might, she could not stop herself from sneezing. The spoon and powder were blown out of her hand and fell behind the commode.

Desperately, she got on her hands and knees, dress ballooning in protest, and reaching behind the commode with a wad of toilet paper, she scraped at the marble floor, trying to scoop up the precious powder.

* * *

The hubbub of gossip echoed through the marble hall as Burstner strolled down the line of women waiting in the hall outside the powder room. A gap of sudden silence followed her like someone running a sponge across the resonating strings of a piano. Sidelong glances from under lowered brows examined her severe man's tuxedo and closely cropped hair. Burstner rather enjoyed the mixture of shock and scorn her fearless independence engendered in the mob of pliant, suppressed women, although a few of them, she was sure, privately felt a grudging admiration.

When she arrived at the powder room door, Burstner had confirmed that the countess was not waiting in line. She pushed her way in, shutting the door against the angry protests of the women in the hall.

The powder room was long and narrow, but the wall of mirrors along one side made it seem wider. Small crystal chandeliers hung over the row of lavatories opposite the three water closets. A Turkish woman was just emerging from the first stall and was shocked to see what she took for a man in the room. But she quickly recognized Burstner's gender, and nodded disdainfully as she exited. Burstner threw open the door of the second stall and revealed a dowager struggling to re-tie the laces on her prodigious girdle. The woman blustered as Burstner put her foot against the girdle's midriff, pulled the laces tight, and tied them for her. "Out, now!" Burstner then commanded.

The dowager rushed away, muttering "Well, I never.... Some people just can't hold their water, I suppose...."

Burstner locked the powder room door from the inside, causing outrage from the women in the hall. She moved to the third and last stall. "Now, dear Olga, it is time for our little chat. We have so much to catch up on."

She threw open the door. There on all fours, her bloomered derrière in the air, was the countess.

Burstner laughed. "So, Olga, I see you have found your place in life at last."

"Oh! You frightened me, Hildy," the countess said, getting up and hurriedly replacing her snuff box and spoon. "I dropped my snuff box. But I have it now. I'd best get back." She started to leave but Burstner pushed her down onto the commode and stood above her.

"So, we Germans are stupid, are we?"

Olga looked up and said, "Oh, Hildy, don't be cross, it was just my little joke. You know I can't resist poking you with a little fun, yes?"

Burstner scowled. "We are on the brink of war and you make jokes!"

Olga looked down, her hands helpless in her lap. "You know I don't understand anything about politics, Hildy. That was always your department."

Burstner snorted. "Ha! That act won't work with me! You made some very passionate speeches about the obsolete aristocracy that summer in Finland, you and your Bolshevik friends."

Olga shook her head sadly. "That was just childish idealism."

"Your passion for social justice certainly didn't prevent you from marrying an elderly count and inheriting his title and fortune."

Olga drew herself up. "Let's say that I have now found my rightful place in society."

Burstner leaned over her, so close her breath moved Olga's hair, and spoke huskily. "Have you forgotten that winter, when you were just a beautiful young actress in Stanislavski's Studio in Moscow, working covertly with your Bolshevik friends to overthrow the czar, and the torrid love affair you had with a certain British officer, and its sad aftermath?"

Olga jerked as if she had been shocked by an electric current.

Burstner reached into her tuxedo jacket and from the inside pocket withdrew a packet of letters bound with a ribbon. "Did you forget that you wrote me all these wonderful letters about the whole sad affair, full of intimate details?"

Olga, stricken, recognized the letters. "I was young and foolish, and he was kind and dashing, and so handsome..." She reached toward the letters, but Burstner jerked them away.

"Wouldn't your noble fans and royal patrons be shocked to learn that the great star, Countess Olga Petrova, was actually – what shall we call it politely – a radical? In both sexual and political matters? As these letters so vividly prove?"

"Hildy!" Olga stood. "You wouldn't!"

"I might. My newspaper could stretch the publication of these letters out for weeks. They would pay a fortune for them."

Olga stared at her old friend. She couldn't help thinking how much Hildy had changed over the years. When Olga, with her broken heart and hopeless pregnancy, had met her in Finland, Hildy had been so tender, so protective, like an older sister. It was Hildy who pulled her through the painful delivery in the foundling home, and the heartbreak of the parting, the brief look at the pretty little baby they wouldn't even let her hold. At least they had let her put her treasured cameo, the one Alfred had given her, in the crib beside her as a final, pitiful gift before she was taken away. Hildy had been so tender in the weeks of her recuperation, they had drawn so close, soul sisters they said, pure love they said; but when Hildy had begun to want more, to consummate their love physically, Olga had been repulsed, had run away, back to Moscow. That was when the change in Hildy had begun, the hardening, the shriveling. Now Hildy was pinched and angular, like a predatory bird, a carrion-eater.

All this ran though Olga's mind. "I am so sorry. You were so good to me," she said.

"I was a fool to love you," Burstner hissed. "You are incapable of loving anyone but yourself."

"No, no, I loved you, Hildy, but not in the way you needed. I loved Alfred, I did. I love him still."

"Bah! Enough of this maudlin nonsense! You are a countess now, you must be rich. You will pay, and pay well, or these letters will be your undoing!"

Olga shook her head, frightened. "No, I am not rich! When the count died, there was some money, yes, but it is gone. I have no head for business. What I didn't squander or give away, I lost on crazy investments. I lost it. All of it."

"You have enough to keep that lover of yours."

Olga gave a painful laugh. "It is not love that ties me to Vittorio. He is not what he seems."

Burstner squinted at her. Could this be true? Could the famous actress, with her jewels and gowns, be a pauper? "But you can always make more, the salaries they pay you…"

"No more! When an actress turns forty, she is finished. There are no more leading roles, and I cannot stoop to be a character woman."

Burstner smiled and slipped the letters back into her jacket. "Well, my dear, you will have to stoop to something. If I do not receive ten thousand pounds before we leave this island, these letters will become a sensation!"

She opened the powder room door and stalked out, ignoring the angry stares of the desperate women who stood in line outside.

* * *

Olga came out of the toilet and, summoning what dignity she could, walked past the impatient women like someone in a trance. Her world, already shaky, was beginning to disintegrate. In the hallway, she felt she was suffocating, needed fresh air. She turned away from the ballroom and rushed out onto the grand terrace.

She ran to the balcony and rested her hands on it, looking out at the moonlit garden, feeling the cool breeze on her face, breathing it in deeply, feeling her pounding heart beginning to slow. She rested there until she was startled by a voice close behind her. "Olya, are you all right?"

Olga turned hopefully to the voice, for it was her beloved Alfred who had first called her by that childlike endearment, "Olya." But she was disappointed. "Oh, Vittorio, it is only you."

Anzilotti stepped beside her. "I came to look for you; you were gone so long I was worried. You look upset."

Olga turned away. "It is nothing. Just an unpleasant encounter with an old friend."

Anzilotti reached out and caressed her hair. "Perhaps you need something to take your mind off it? A little pick-me-up?"

Olga was torn. She knew she had to somehow tear herself away from his influence, but she hadn't the strength. Every fiber of her body was crying out for a "pick-me-up." And now this business of the letters…. She turned to him. "Yes, I need some, please. I lost all I had left just now in the powder room."

They both failed to notice that Burstner was lurking just inside the French doors. She had seen Anzilotti going out onto the terrace and had followed him. Now she watched intently as Anzilotti took a small vial out of his pocket and dangled it in front of the countess' nose.

The countess followed the vial with her eyes like a subject watching a hypnotist's watch. Anzilotti whispered, "This is a special treat that has just arrived from the mainland. Better, *cara mia,* far better than that dung you've been using lately."

Olga snatched at the vial, but Anzilotti pulled it back. "No, no, *cara mia*, not here. You know that oaf of a governor would just love an excuse to toss me out on my ass." Vittorio smiled and slipped the vial back into his pocket. "Now off you go, back to your admiring public. I'll meet you inside."

Olga trembled, but pulled herself up with difficulty and moved away.

Watching her go, Anzilotti's smile faded and he muttered under his breath, "*Vaca*! *Putana*!"

Burstner pulled back into the shadows as Olga rushed past. She thought, This could be useful. Now I have them both. She slipped away toward the ballroom.

Anzilotti lit a cigarette and rested against the balustrade. How tired he felt! Entertaining the countess was exhausting in so many ways: physically, given her insatiable sexual appetite and penchant for athletic positions, and spiritually, given her constant need for reassurance. He had always fancied younger women, and as he grew older he preferred them even younger, the younger the better. Like that harpsichord player, or even that American. *O Dio*, what a chest she had! With someone like that, Vittorio thought, he could again feel the stirring in his loins from whence had come his poetic inspiration.

But sad to say, it had been many years since pen or penis had been at their best, and his flaccid poetic output had emptied his coffers. Now he was reduced to living off rich women of a certain age, and he dreaded the day when advancing age disqualified him from even that sordid existence. Already, as he could feel with his own fingers, the skin of his throat was beginning to hang like an old lady's loose gown. He was mere millimeters away from wattles.

Vittorio was so consumed with these dire ruminations that he almost failed to notice that one of the subjects of his lust, Shirley Benton, had wandered out onto the terrace. She was at the other end of the balustrade looking out over the garden when he saw her.

Vittorio snubbed out his cigarette, adjusted the drape of his jacket, rubbed a palm across his hair to smooth it, and nonchalantly walked over to her. In his most sonorous tones, he said, "Ah, Mrs. Benton. I hoped I might see you alone, but I didn't think it would be this soon."

Shirley turned and peered at him in the moonlight, squinting as nearsighted people do. "Oh?" she said. "I don't believe I've had the pleasure...."

"Permit me to introduce myself. I am Vittorio Anzilotti." Then, as if presenting his credentials as a lover, he added, "I am Italian."

Shirley smiled. "Well, we don't see many Eyetalians back in Kansas, but I had guessed as much. I'm pleased to meet you, Mr. Anzilotti." She extended her hand, and instead of shaking it, Vittorio took it in his, bowed, and kissed it, holding the kiss several seconds longer than mere politeness required. Shirley giggled, "Oh my, that's another thing we don't do in Kansas."

As Vittorio straightened, his eyes swept across her bosom like a farmer admiring a fertile field. He looked deeply into her eyes and said, "I'm sure there are many things you don't do in Kansas that you may have an opportunity to do here in Europe, Mrs. Benton."

Shirley blushed and turned away to look out over the gardens. "How beautiful it is here. I've never seen anything like it before."

"What a shame. But now you are on your honeymoon and can do all the sightseeing you want."

"Well, I'd like to, but John has a lot of duties, meetings and all."

Vittorio took her arm and guided her along the balustrade. "If the lieutenant is too busy, Mrs. Benton, I would be happy to show you the sights of the island if you would like." He stopped and swept his arm across the view. "I know every inch of it. I've been coming here for years. I am a poet, and here, one is surrounded by constant reminders of heroic antiquity, echoes of a time of grandeur and pagan worship, of the building of empires, of erotic passion on an epic scale!" Vittorio gestured at the ancient statues that surrounded the terrace, and in particular one of Diana. Vittorio pointed up at it. "I think that you are secretly just like her. She was called Artemis by the Greeks, then worshipped in Rome as Diana the huntress, and in the middle ages she became the Queen of Witches, the mistress of majick."

"Yes," Shirley said softly, "That is what I want. Magic. I've heard that this place has magical properties, that on the island of dreams you can have magical experiences." Shirley surprised Vittorio by leaning close so their foreheads were nearly touching. Like a young girl telling dark secrets she whispered, "I want to try some magic. I'm told that you can help. That you dispense magic potions."

Vittorio's pulse quickened. Perhaps this American farm girl was not so naïve as he had assumed. He took her hand. "I am at your command. You need only ask and I will do anything in my power to satisfy you."

"Well," Shirley said, "I'd like to try some."

"Here!" Vittorio led her into the shadow behind the statue. He slipped his hand into his jacket and showed her the little golden vial. "This is the magic lantern of the Arabian tales. There is a genie within who can show you a whole new universe of infinite delights. It would give me the greatest pleasure to let you rub the lantern and see your wish granted."

Shirley took it in her hand and turned it slowly, fascinated, then frowned. "John would be very upset if he found out."

"It will be our secret, I promise." Vittorio opened it for her and sprinkled some powder onto the back of his hand. "John will never know."

Shirley moistened a finger and dipped it tentatively into the powder, tasted it, and smiled. She lowered her head and licked the back of his hand clean. The feel of her tongue on his skin made Vittorio tremble like a schoolboy. Perhaps she might… and on her honeymoon! What a conquest that would be! What a story to tell his cronies in Rome!

She looked up at him, her eyes sparkling. "That is quite something," she said. "Is there a lot of this on the island?"

"As much as one could wish for," Vittorio said.

"Is it expensive?"

"There is a cost, but the experiences it provides are beyond price."

Shirley reached into her little purse and produced a roll of bills. "I have some of my own money. Would this be enough?"

Vittorio took the bills. A quick glance confirmed that they were of large denominations. Vittorio felt a surge of excitement. "Enough for now, assuredly." He gave her the vial. "There is more whenever you like."

She deposited the vial in her purse. "And where does it come from?"

Vittorio chuckled. "From my magic helpers."

"Oh, you're just making fun of me," Shirley said, pouting.

"No, no, I assure you. I have acolytes, apprentice sorcerers you might say."

"Prove it," Shirley said petulantly, "or I shan't believe you."

Vittorio put his finger to his lips and led her to the far side of the terrace above the kitchen's back door and pointed down. "There, you can see them for yourself."

Excited as a child, she leaned over and looked. There on the loading dock below, Makarios and Stefano were lifting the last of the crates from the last shipment of produce. They looked up and Makarios scowled at Vittorio. He came to the edge of the wall below them and whispered, "We have unfinished business, Vittorio. Time is running out."

"All will be well, I assure you," Vittorio whispered back. "Look," he flashed the roll of bills and gestured toward Shirley with his head, "we have initiated yet another member of our magic circle."

Shirley gave a little wave.

* * *

The harbor was quiet and deserted. The old man cut the engine and let his boat glide effortlessly into its customary slip. He tossed his bow painter expertly over the cleat. He had no sooner hauled the line taut than his passenger leapt soundlessly onto the dock and disappeared into the maze of portside alleys. As he passed the little town church, he heard the murmur of worshippers saying a novena.

At the appointed place, a motorcycle sat waiting. Streisel tucked his slouch hat into his coat, put on the leather helmet and goggles hanging from the handlebars, then mounted and started the engine. He roared away up the twisting road that led to Nicosia and the embassy.

Meanwhile, the old fisherman made the line fast and settled atop a pile of nets on his afterdeck. He took from the portside locker a bottle of Retsina, a block of pungent cheese, a slab of rough, dark bread, and a fresh, ripe pear. He settled down to enjoy this late supper, prepared for the indeterminate wait that he had been warned might pass before the courier's return, when Streisel would have to be returned to the patrol boat as quickly as possible.

THIRD COURSE: THE FISH

7. Olga's Sole

When the intermission had begun and Shirley had joined the rush of women moving toward the toilets, John stayed behind, entranced by a Bach fugue that Lydia was playing. Not a music lover by nature, John was nonetheless captivated by the emotional quality with which Lydia endowed the piece. What was it that so fascinated him, he wondered? Surely it was the intensity of purpose, even the sheer *will* he heard in every note, so perfect an expression of both the nearly demonic drive of Bach and the harsh, plucking action of the harpsichord itself, an action that required a tremendous commitment to every keystroke. It was this implacable will that he could recognize and understand; it touched an important part of him, a part that his own dear, soft, naïve wife would probably never know existed. He found himself staring at Lydia as she attacked the keyboard, feeling in his own body the rhythmic actions of hers. At one point she looked up and met his eyes, and their communion became so personal, so – yes, sexual – that John felt his manhood rise.

Suddenly aware that Mustafa Ataturk was looking at him with a knowing smirk, John looked away from Lydia and excused himself from the table, saying, "I guess I'd better find Shirley. No telling what mischief she might be getting into."

"Yes, by all means," Ataturk smiled, "do find your charming wife and bring her back to us."

Moving through the hallway, scanning the dwindling line of women leading to the toilets, John was aware of the sensation he was causing among the diplomatic wives aflutter over the appearance of someone so young and handsome in their midst. When he came out onto the terrace, he thought at first that it was empty, but then saw Shirley leaning over the side balustrade, and next to her that Anzilotti fellow with his arm around her! It looked almost as if she were being sick, as she had been during the voyage to the island, spending hours hunched over the railing. He called to her, "Shirley, are you all right?"

Shirley spun around. It took her a moment to focus on him. "John?"

He approached her. "What have you been doing out here so long?"

"Oh, John, Mr. Anzilotti has just been telling me about the wonderful statues and everything."

Anzilotti moved away from Shirley and bowed stiffly. John frowned. "I didn't think you cared for this sort of thing."

Vittorio turned to Shirley. "I must get back to the countess. I have very much enjoyed meeting you, Mrs. Benton. I do hope you like the rest of your stay on the island." He bowed, then nodded to John, "Lieutenant Benton," and hurried away.

John watched him go. His expression darkened. "You really must be more careful around these people, Shirley. The governor says he has a very unsavory reputation."

"Really? He seemed awfully nice. He told me about the history of the island. It's all so wonderful. Did you know it was first settled 1600 years before Christ? And that it was a Greek kingdom after that?"

"Why this sudden interest?" John asked.

"Well," Shirley gushed, "all those archeological sites. I thought Mr. Carnegie would want us to learn more about it, seeing as how he's so keen on all that stuff."

John shook his head. "I don't think Mr. Carnegie needs our help in that department, darling. I want you to stay away from Anzilotti, understood?"

"I just want to help. I'm so afraid I'm going to spoil things for you here."

John patted her hair. "All you have to do is smile and be your own charming self. Everyone here has fallen in love with you at first sight, just like I did."

Shirley took a deep breath. "You're so good to me, John. Sometimes I can't believe how lucky we've been; it's so romantic here. I couldn't think of a better honeymoon."

He kissed her on the forehead and said, "I feel the same way."

Governor Woodford opened one of the French doors. "Ah, Lieutenant and Mrs. Benton, here you are. I'm sorry to interrupt the honeymooners, but I wonder if I might have a word with the lieutenant in private. It won't take long, we have only a few minutes before the fish is served."

The two Americans turned to him and John said, "Certainly, governor, Shirley was just going back to the table."

Shirley pouted, but said, "Yes, of course." She started to leave, then stopped and curtsied to Woodford. "Awfully nice place, Your Excellency."

Woodford smiled as she bustled away. "Delightful woman you have there, John."

John looked after Shirley, bemused. "Not a dull moment. I never know what she'll do next."

Woodford took his arm and guided him back toward the study. "You've only been married a few weeks, I take it?"

"Yes, it all happened rather suddenly. I had just gotten my posting here, and I was invited to a weekend at the Carnegie mansion in Pittsburgh, and she was one of the houseguests. To make a short story even shorter, we were married just weeks later! I suppose it was rather impetuous...."

Woodford smiled. "One must follow one's heart, lad. I could tell you a few tales of my own youth...." They arrived at the study door and Woodford gestured for John to enter. "But I'm afraid we have more serious matters to discuss."

Once they were inside, Woodford carefully locked the door. He leveled a serious gaze on John. "As you know, Lieutenant, tensions between the two great alliances of Europe have been building for some time, and this assassination of the Archduke has brought things to a head."

John nodded. "Yes, my government is watching the situation with keen interest. But for now, we regard it as a local dispute between Austria and Serbia."

Woodford shook his head gravely. "I wish that was all it was, but it will not remain a local matter. If Austria attacks, all of Europe will soon be drawn in. Eventually, perhaps even the United States."

With characteristic American optimism, John said, "But surely this can all be resolved before it comes to that...."

Woodford raised a hand. "So we hope." He went to his desk and from a locked drawer withdrew a diplomatic pouch.

Speaking nearly in a whisper, he went on, "What I am about to show you is a crucial government document. I must swear you to complete secrecy. Are you prepared to guard this secret with your life, on your honor as an officer and a gentleman?"

"Of course," John said at once, eyeing Woodford's Victoria Cross. "You can be sure of my discretion."

"Good," Woodford said. He opened the pouch and removed a document with an ornate seal. "This, Lieutenant, arrived only this afternoon. It is a secret treaty struck by the Allies at the urging of the British Foreign Office. I cannot tell you what it contains, but it is our last hope to avert war. The Austrians are sending a courier who will confirm the validity of this treaty. My task, Lieutenant Benton, is to see it safely delivered to that courier."

"When will he arrive?" John asked.

"I can't be sure. The courier could be anyone – even one of the guests already here – and the contact might occur at any time. Therefore, I shall have to carry the treaty with me for the remainder of the evening. And that is why I need your help."

Woodford went to the sideboard and poured them both glasses of whiskey. He went on. "There are so many double agents at work on all sides that I daresay you could not throw a stone in the dining room tonight without hitting a spy or two. As a result, not much that happens in the diplomatic world remains secret for long, so I must assume that word of the treaty and its presence here is known and some effort may be made to intercept it. I can trust no one, not even those on my own staff. As an American, Lieutenant, you are virtually the only one here with no vested interest in this matter, and I need an able-bodied man I can trust. I shall appreciate it if you will stand ready to assist should anything untoward occur."

John stepped forward and took one of the glasses. "You can count on me, sir." He raised it, and they toasted.

Woodford said, "These are passionate people my lad, and there are those who would destroy the treaty if they could." He carefully slipped the treaty under his cummerbund. "Europe is a powder keg, Lieutenant, and just now, *we* are the fuse."

* * *

Another Olga dish! Woodford had insisted on including the two creations that the great Escoffier had named in honor of the countess. Poor Makarios had dug up a dog-eared copy of Escoffier's *Guide Culinaire* and was doing his best to follow the instructions, but the terse recipes assumed more knowledge than the poor Cypriot possessed. The recipe for the fish mentioned a *fumet* and *sauce Mornay*, about the making of which Makarios could only guess. And nowhere did Escoffier mention cooking times or temperatures! The dishes Makarios could produce would be only rough approximations of the originals.

Nicky had assured his cousin that since no one in the embassy, Woodford included, had ever tasted the originals, they wouldn't notice the difference. "But the countess herself?" Makarios had said. "She will know the difference!"

Nicky had shaken his head. "We will be very generous with her champagne. Besides, she will be so flattered that it would be unthinkable for her to complain. Trust me."

Fillets of Sole Olga

Bake beforehand, in the oven, as many fine well-washed potatoes as there are fillets of sole. As soon as they are done, remove a piece of the baked shell and withdraw the pulp to leave nothing but the long, parched shells. Fold the fillets and poach them with a little excellent fish fumet. Garnish the bottom of each prepared shell with a tablespoon of shelled shrimp tails, combined with a white-wine sauce.

Put a poached fillet of sole upon this garnish; cover with sufficient Mornay sauce to completely fill each shell; sprinkle with grated cheese and glaze quickly. Put on a napkin the moment the fillets have been taken from the oven, and serve immediately.

There was chaos in the kitchen. The fish course was the most delicate and demanding of the entire meal. It had to be served immediately after it came out of the oven, but one of the boys had spilled an entire tray of potato shells. There was no time to bake another batch from scratch, so the damaged shells had to be repaired and disguised with a hastily prepared decoration of *Pommes Anna* squeezed through a pastry tube. This was being done as Nicky left the desperate cooks to their work and stepped through the kitchen doors into the butler's pantry leading to the dining room.

He stepped around the partition that separated the dining area from the pantry and signaled to Lydia, who was taking advantage of the long break to eat a little. She excused herself from the table and met him at the service partition. "What's wrong?" she asked, though if she was at all nervous, she showed no outward sign, and Nicky marveled at her icy control.

"Trouble with the fish. We need you to kill some time. Play something."

"But everything is still set to go?"

"Everything. Just wait for my signal."

Lydia gave him a quick kiss and went back to her table at the rear of the dining room.

"Time to go back to work, I'm afraid," she explained to her dinner companions. "Any requests?"

Burstner said, "Anything from opera, but German, of course."

Vittorio wrinkled his nose and countered with, "Yes, opera, please, but Puccini, or Verdi!"

Lydia nodded. "Opera it is." She went up to the harpsichord. In the spirit of neutrality she began to play the overture from Bizet's *Carmen,* with a nod to both Burstner and Anzilotti. Looking down from the stage, she could see across to the head table, where Woodford and the American lieutenant were just sitting down. He's a handsome one, she thought, wasted on that pasty wife. And what had passed between them during the Bach – well, there was something about this American that intrigued and alerted her. He would bear watching.

* * *

In the kitchen, Makarios and his cooks were working at a fever pitch. Some five minutes passed, during which Makarios aged ten years, but finally the potato skins were repaired, filled, and browning under the salamanders. At last they were all arranged on serving trays and whisked into the dining room.

Lydia, who had by then been playing for over ten minutes, was so relieved when the waiters emerged with the trays that she struck up *The March of the Toreadors*.

The countess was overjoyed when she saw the fish. "Oh, my," she exclaimed happily, "it's the other dish Escoffier dedicated to me! This is really too, too much!"

Burstner grumbled and thought, Yes, it certainly is. Woodford is making a fool of himself all over again.

Vittorio explored his portion with a fork and said, "I shouldn't think Escoffier intended the sole to be smothered in quite this much potato."

The countess drew herself up, protective of her namesake, just as Nicky had foretold. "But he did, I assure you. This is just how he did it!" She gestured to Nicky. "Tell the chef that Monsieur Escoffier couldn't have done better himself!"

Nicky bowed and said, "He will be delighted to hear that, countess."

The wine stewards were already pouring the splendid Montrachet 1909 that Woodford had selected for the fish. When the sole arrived at the head table Shirley exclaimed, "Oh, look, John, its little potato boats, just like back home!" She took a bite and frowned. "Oh, but they have fish inside."

John explained to the table, "Shirley doesn't like fish."

Shirley brightened and said, "I'll just scrape the fish out. The potato skins are really very good by themselves."

Woodford tasted the fish thoughtfully. He waved to Nicky, who trotted over. "Yes, my lord?"

"Did I see you speaking with the countess?"

"Yes, my lord. She wished to compliment the chef on the fish. Said Escoffier himself couldn't have done better."

"Well, that's wonderful. But that was rather a long wait between the soup and the fish, Nicky. Any trouble in the kitchen?'

"Just a temporary setback, sir, everything's back to normal."

"Well," Woodford said, "I know this is quite a challenge for the boys. Perhaps they might appreciate a little encouragement." He dabbed his mouth with his napkin and pushed himself back from the table.

Nicky wasn't eager for Woodford to stick his nose into the kitchen, but there was nothing he could say without arousing suspicion. Woodford bowed to his guests. "If you all will excuse me, I'll be back in a moment." As he left, he leaned close to John and whispered, "Keep a weather eye."

"Will do," John answered.

Shirley swallowed a mouthful of potato skins and asked, "Are you sure everything is all right, John? Everyone seems kind of on edge...."

John said rather too sharply, "It's all right, dear, I can handle it."

Nicky noticed the momentary expression of hurt that flashed across Shirley's face, but a moment later she had covered it with her vacuous smile. Nicky bowed toward them and said, "Mr. and Mrs. Benton, I trust you are enjoying our island thus far?"

John looked up at him. "Yes, thank you.... I'm afraid I don't remember your name...."

Nicky bowed. "Phocas, Nicephorus Phocas. But everyone just calls me Nicky."

Shirley took a sip of her wine and said, "I just love your native costumes. Do you dress like this all the time?"

Nicky smiled. "Only when we have charming guests from America."

Shirley giggled.

John was not amused. There was something about Nicky that alerted John to danger— not over this harmless flirtation, that was just continental courtesy, but something more threatening. Nicky reminded him of working class men he knew at home, men who made a show of politeness but who in their hearts were so full of rage and self-pity that – usually in the name of some crackpot ideology – they plotted and schemed and were apt to throw bombs, as they had at the Haymarket Riot. John wondered if Woodford knew he had a potential traitor in his midst? No, John thought, Woodford is like so many of the political leaders back home, the sort of men who think well of the world and everyone in it until they are proven wrong, usually when it is too late.

John rose and spoke to Shirley. "Excuse me, dear, I need to ask Nicky here something. I'll be right back."

Shirley took another sip of wine and looked over at the sultan's emissary. "Fine, I'll just talk to Mr. Ataturk while you're gone. There's a lot I'd like to learn about Turkey. I have oodles of questions!"

Mustafa Ataturk nodded and said, "I shall do my best to enlighten you, Mrs. Benton." He smiled a sickly smile, girding his loins for the onslaught he knew Shirley was about to unleash.

* * *

John led Nicky resolutely through the foyer. Stefano, on duty at the top of the stairs, glanced toward Nicky, his eyes asking what was going on. Nicky shook his head and gestured toward John with a shrug.

Without slowing down, John headed for the front door, saying, "Let's step outside a moment."

On the front porch, John confirmed that they were alone and turned to Nicky. "You are in charge of the household here?"

There was something about the way the American asked the question that put Nicky on edge. Nicky had noticed the quick familiarity that had sprung up between Woodford and the young lieutenant, and it made him wary. Unfortunately, nervousness had always made Nicky talk too much. He answered, "The governor needed someone who spoke Italian, Turkish, and Greek who could deal with the tradesmen and native staff."

John read Nicky's nervousness, and could see a bead of perspiration on the overseer's upper lip. He was now convinced that this man was hiding something, perhaps something important. He asked, "You were born on Cyprus?"

Nicky said, "Yes, and my father and grandfather and many generations before them."

"And yet," John went on, "I understand that most Cypriots want to ally the island with Greece. I notice that you have a Greek name."

Nicky knew that he should avoid being drawn into an argument with the American, but he could not resist pulling himself up to his full height and announcing, "I was named for a Byzantine emperor. And like most of us on the island, yes, I consider myself Greek. I freely admit that I want our nation to be reunited with the mother country."

John was intrigued by this unsubmissive servant. He decided to see how far he could push him and said, "Well, you can hardly call yourselves a nation, can you? You've never been independent, I believe."

John's aim was true. Nicky's face reddened. "No, we haven't. For three thousand years we have been dominated by outsiders. And now you Americans come."

John laughed, making sure that his voice had a dismissive tone. "My good man, America has no territorial claim here."

Nicky took the bait. "You don't need our territory, you just take whatever you want from it." Nicky's passion was getting the best of him, and he went on hotly, "For twelve years, the American consul before you dug like a man possessed. What antiquities the Turks and British hadn't already taken, he shipped by the boatload back to New York. Our most priceless treasures ended up in Mr. Carnegie's hoard in your Metropolitan Museum."

At the mention of Carnegie, John drew the line. He pointed a finger at Nicky and said, "I'm sure Mr. Carnegie was acting in accord with your laws—"

"Laws? Whose laws?" Nicky had gone too far to back down now. "Ottoman law? Two-thirds to the digger, one-third to the Turkish government? Nothing to us! And the black market in Cypriot art is enormous. Your Mr. Carnegie has his poachers everywhere!"

John thrust his face close to Nicky's. "Now, see here! I happen to know Mr. Carnegie personally and I will not have you insulting him. He is a fine man with a real concern for your people, and he always pays a fair price —"

Nicky pushed up against John. He kept his voice down, but his intensity showed in the raised cords of his neck. "Money? Why is it always money with you Americans? What do you know of our people? We are farmers and ranchers, easy to subdue. And so gullible. When the British came 40 years ago, we welcomed them as liberators. But they have their own, subtle forms of oppression. My mother worked here in this embassy. For twenty years she scrubbed these marble floors until she could no longer walk. My father worked in the British asbestos mines until he could no longer breathe. And now you come, with your Carnegie money. But we will take back what is ours!"

A demure cough startled the two men. They turned to see Lydia standing in the doorway. "I'm sorry," she said, "I was coming out for a breath of air and I heard voices. I was afraid there was something wrong." When she had noticed John and Nicky leaving the dining room, she had ended a piece quickly and had hurried after them, seized by a premonition of trouble. She was glad she had arrived in time to extricate Nicky and prevent anything from getting out of hand.

John tugged his uniform jacket taut and stepped toward her. "It's all right, Miss Seymour. Just a difference of political opinion."

Lydia nodded. "I understand," she smiled, "affairs of state." She glanced at Nicky and with a slight gesture of her eyes signaled him to leave.

"If you will excuse me, I must return to my duties," Nicky said.

John turned back to Nicky. "You can be sure I shall inform your employer of your concerns."

Nicky bowed coldly, and without another word, went inside.

"What an unpleasant man," Lydia said, looking after Nicky. "He frightens me. You can never tell what he's thinking."

John turned to her. "I know exactly what he is thinking, Miss Seymour. There are thousands like him; the have-nots who want to be given their share without working for it. We have them at home, too, the Wobblies and their ilk. And now, the Bolsheviks are spreading their infernal gospel all over the world."

Lydia laughed softly. "You sound just like Governor Woodford."

John turned to her. The light from the doorway accentuated her fine features and figure. He smiled. "I take that as a compliment." They moved down the stairs under the *port-cochere* and strolled onto the lawn at the front of the embassy.

"Oh, the governor is very sweet," Lydia continued, "but terribly old-fashioned. Old School tie, the Regiment, and all that."

John said, "There's a lot of good in tradition, Miss Seymour. There are entirely too many people like Nicky running around who'd rather carry a bomb than a shovel. They have to be watched. Like wild dogs, they are dangerous when they band together."

Lydia turned and put a hand on John's lapel. "Well, I'm sure that men like you and the governor and Mr. Carnegie can keep them in line."

John was flattered. "Actually, I'm quite new at the game myself, but yes, the established order is the only alternative to chaos. *'Après moi, le deluge,'* as they say." They both laughed, John at his own wit, Lydia because his French was truly terrible.

John went on, "The governor mentioned this tour of yours...."

Lydia was rapturous. "Yes, it's been wonderful! I've visited all sorts of exotic places, nearly the whole empire." She sighed. "It's been a lifesaver, really; I grew up in an orphanage, never knew my parents. My life was frightfully empty, but then I found my music. It has given me a sense of purpose." She gazed up into his eyes. "But I'm sure a man like you understands that, Lieutenant Benton."

John swallowed. He felt as if he were falling into those bottomless blue eyes. "Yes, certainly. And please, call me John."

Lydia moved even closer to him. "I've met the most interesting people, John, though I do get homesick and lonely at times. It's not easy for a young girl alone in the world...."

John could smell the lilac scent of her perfume. He floated on it. "I'm sure it's not. But you have your music, at least. And I must say you play beautifully. I am no expert, but I could sense an extraordinary power in your playing."

Lydia wished that she were capable of blushing, but she did the best she could by lowering her eyes and smiling demurely. "I am so pleased that you liked it."

"I more than liked it," John said. "It thrilled me like no music has before."

They had stopped some ten yards from the front steps and were standing very close. The moment seemed full of promise. John was about to say more when Nicky's voice cut through the night: "Lieutenant Benton."

John and Lydia moved quickly apart. Nicky had appeared silently from the door and was looking down from the porch.

"The governor asks that you join him in his study as soon as possible."

"Certainly," John said, then turned and bowed sharply to Lydia. "Miss Seymour, you will excuse me?"

Lydia smiled. "Of course, Lieutenant."

John started up the stairs and, with a baleful glance at Nicky, went inside.

As soon as John was gone, Lydia whirled on Nicky. "What the hell were you doing, arguing with him like that? If I hadn't come along you would have given everything away."

Nicky was angry too. "And what were you doing making eyes at him? If I hadn't come along, I think you might have given more than our plan away!"

Lydia glared. "I don't trust him. He's up to something and I was trying to find out what. This is no time for jealousy! Now get hold of yourself. I have to get back."

She stormed up the stairs. Nicky watched her go. He had never felt such jealousy before. What was happening to him? He tried to focus on what he had to do tonight. Whatever else, he mustn't let Father Demetrius and the others down.

* * *

Inside, John was heading for the study when Burstner came suddenly out of the library and intercepted him. He nodded and tried to move past, but she held up her hand, in which she was carrying a small, sealed envelope, which she handed him. "Would you be a good fellow and give the governor this note for me? Take special care that the seal is not broken."

John took it and nodded. "Of course, Fraulein."

As Burstner moved away and out the front door, John watched her go, thinking that from the rear you could easily mistake her for a man; her movements were athletic, but not graceful. Yet there was an unmistakable aura of mystery about her. And she was German. John looked thoughtfully at the note she had given him. Well, he thought, we'll find out soon enough.

* * *

Streisel saw the lights of the city approaching. He slowed the motorcycle as he passed through the outskirts and moved through the western gate. He was puzzled by the apparent emptiness of the streets. Even the taverns seemed deserted. As he passed the cathedral, he remembered that he had seen people gathered in the church at Kyrenia. It must be some saint's day, he thought.

He had been carefully briefed on the layout of the town and continued toward the Plaza Santa Isabel. There he killed the engine and rolled the motorcycle out of sight in the darkness behind one of the buildings. He removed the leather helmet and goggles and restored his slouch hat. The clock in the town hall was just chiming ten as he lit a cigarette and settled down to wait for his next contact. Just two hours to go.

FOURTH COURSE: THE ENTRÉES

8.   Little Pieces of Small Birds

True to the grand culinary tradition, the banquet had two main meat courses. First came the *entrées*, which served as an introduction to the more substantial *relevé* that would follow. Woodford had decided to serve two *entrées,* a light game dish and a cold lamb, to be followed by a robust *relevé* of roast beef.

For the game entrée, Woodford had organized a hunt. Early the previous morning, he and several of his houseguests, guided by Nicky, had trudged into the still-dew-covered fields to shoot. Though many were military men, it was Nicky, who had grown up in this countryside with a gun against his shoulder, who bagged a quantity of the elusive ortolan, a small brownish bird similar to the English bobolink. These had been prepared in the Turkish style in honor of the sultan, with each of the birds poached over a truffled forcemeat. Escoffier called these little birds *sylphides*, named for the elemental beings who, like the birds themselves, inhabited the forests and lived on air. It was a dish that depended on perfect timing, and so had given Makarios nightmares.

Sylphides of Ortolans

Butter some very small porcelain or silver cassolettes, and fill them half-full with mousseline forcemeat of ortolans prepared with truffle essence.

Set these cassolettes in the oven, that the forcemeat may cook. Cook in butter, for three minutes only, as many whole ortolans as there are garnished cassolettes, and proceed so as to have them just ready when the forcemeat is done cooking.

Place an ortolan in each cassolette and sprinkle them with nut brown butter, combined with a little pale melted glaze and pineapple juice.

Lydia decided to play, as a private joke, music from *Swan Lake* during what she thought of as "the bird course." The stewards poured the magnificent, earthy and full-bodied *Chateau Rothschild 1892* that accompanied the game.

In the Mediterranean tradition, the ortolans were served with the heads still attached. When the dishes were laid down, Shirley took one look at the pathetic heads hanging limp and cried out, "Oh, the poor little things!" She covered her mouth with her napkin and had to excuse herself hurriedly, to the secret amusement and relief of many.

At the rear table, the countess, who also looked suddenly unwell, hurriedly took her leave and rushed through the dining room toward the terrace.

* * *

After the little birds were served, Makarios took a well-earned break for a cigarette at the back door of the kitchen. The most difficult dishes had been successfully completed. Of the remaining courses, the roasts and salad were mostly pre-prepared. Only the dessert remained as a challenge, and that for an entirely different reason.

Makarios leaned against the door of the loading dock, which was situated at one side below the grand terrace. He inhaled, savoring the bits of hashish he had rolled into his cigarette. All in all, despite the extravagance of Woodford's menu, this had been a very successful and profitable evening. He and Stefano had just made an entirely new arrangement for their growing cocaine and art smuggling operation with a most unlikely but extremely generous client, and they would be glad to be done with the irresponsible and erratic Italian. Thanks to their new partner, they had enough ready cash to leave the embassy and Nicosia for good and to set up a new headquarters somewhere on the coast, where deliveries would be easier. And with the money Vittorio owed, Makarios could at last buy that sailboat he had his eye on. Of course, if Vittorio failed to pay his debt, they would have to make an example of him before leaving – but that would be easy under cover of the rebellion Nicky and Father Demetrius had so conveniently provided.

Yes, Makarios thought, inhaling deeply, life was good, and would soon be even better.

* * *

Vittorio put a cautionary finger to Olga's nose. "This new 'treat' is considerably more expensive than what you've been consuming for the past several weeks, countess. In all, you owe me nearly five thousand pounds. First pay, then you can have more."

The countess clung to him, imploring. "Oh, Vittorio, I will pay you somehow, I swear. My jewels," she cried, "would you accept those?"

Vittorio scoffed, "Bah! Paste from the costume department! Fake, like everything about you...." In disgust he pushed her away.

The countess fell against the balustrade, then onto the marble floor. She sat against the railing, rubbing her wrist and sobbing. "How dare you! I am a great artist...."

Vittorio stood over her, snarling, "You were a competent ingénue with a knack for seducing directors. But you cannot play Ophelia forever."

The countess looked up with sudden loathing. "You did this to me, you Italian devil! You and your cocaine.... I'll be revenged somehow, I swear it!"

Vittorio knelt beside her. "You are in no position to threaten anyone." Seeing that they were still alone, he grabbed her arm and bent it back, none too gently. In an urgent whisper he said, "And you must pay tonight! You have no idea what will happen if I fail to make my payment. My business associates have an unpleasant and permanent way of assessing late penalties on their contracts!"

"But how, tonight?" Olga pleaded.

"I will tell you how. There is a fortune in precious gems sitting in your old lover's safe at this very moment."

"The tribute?"

"Yes, the tribute. And you will persuade Woodford to give you a few of the stones. They will hardly be missed."

"But why would he do that?"

"You will appeal to his great love for you."

Her eyes glistened. "That was so long ago...."

"Bah! He loves you still. A blind man could see it. Why do you think he chose half the dishes in this dinner in your honor? You will tell him that it is a matter of life and death. Because believe me, dear Olga, it is! For both of us!"

He pushed her away and was gone.

Alone, the countess pulled herself to her feet. Looking over the balustrade into the darkness below, she momentarily thought of throwing herself over and ending the torment forever. For a long moment, her self-loathing battled with her fear of death.

At last, her love of life reasserted itself. "What has he done to me?" she whispered to herself. "But I must get that money.... Oh, Alfy, forgive me for what I must do."

* * *

Just after sunset, the partisans had gathered in the forest at the base of the hill. For the past two hours, they had moved slowly, silently, up the hill toward the embassy. Now they waited in the underbrush on the steep hillside that came right up to the verge of the embassy gardens. Already, advance parties had crept onto the grounds, waved ahead by Stefano and their compatriots in the house guard, and were huddled in the dark grottos beneath the embassy's terraces.

Barely daring to breathe, they sat gripping their weapons, some methodically cleaning already immaculate rifles and shotguns, staring into the darkness, each of them alone with their thoughts as they contemplated the possibilities of freedom and death.

* * *

Woodford was alone in his study. The heavy drapes over one of the large windows had been drawn back, exposing a mesh enclosure built into the casement, extending out several feet from the side of the building. Woodford was about to open the enclosure when there was a knock, and he went to the door. "Yes? Who is it?"

From outside, John answered, "Lieutenant Benton."

"Are you alone?"

"Yes."

"Just a moment." Woodford unlocked the door and opened it just enough for John to enter. "Come in, quickly."

John hurried in as Woodford closed and locked the door. "You sent for me?"

"Yes, I have received a signal."

John heard cooing from the wire enclosure at the window. "What in the world...?"

Woodford went to the window and opened a small door in the enclosure.

"There is a radio in the barracks below," Woodford explained. "But our radio messages are easily intercepted, and we cannot be sure our codes are secure. This," he said, lifting a white carrier pigeon from the coop, "is our most secret means of communication with the mainland. Each week, some of these pigeons are taken by ship to our outpost in the Palestine. From there, they can be released as needed to carry diplomatic signals to us here. When they pass through the doorway into the coop, a signal light flashes. This one has just arrived. Let us see what message it carries."

Woodford held the bird gently on its back. Trained to be handled in this way, the bird was quiet. Woodford nodded toward a small silver capsule on its leg. "It helps if there are two of us," he said.

John took his cue and removed the capsule from the bird. Woodford immediately returned the bird to the coop, closed the window, and drew the heavy drapes closed.

"Now, let us see what we have." Back at the desk, John watched as Woodford opened the capsule and removed a tiny roll of paper. He smoothed it out on the blotter and took a large magnifying glass from the drawer. Bending close, he read for a moment, then rose gravely.

"This tells me that the Austrian courier is already on the island. I am to meet him at midnight by the statue of Athena in the center of the garden maze. Things are coming to a head. Serbia has sent a surprisingly conciliatory response to Austria, but it has been rejected. The Austrian army has mobilized along the Serbian border. It appears that an invasion will commence immediately upon the expiration of the deadline."

Woodford dropped the message into the fireplace and watched it curl and burn. "That, I fear," he said quietly, watching the flames, "will be the fate of Europe if we fail." He turned to John and patted his cummerbund. "This treaty is now the last hope."

"I almost forgot," John said, taking the note from Burstner from his pocket. "This is for you."

Woodford tore it open. He looked up. "It asks for a private meeting concerning 'an affair of state.' " He thought for a moment. "You don't suppose that Burstner could be the courier? A German journalist – it would be a good cover." He dropped the note into the fire. "There is only one way to find out."

* * *

As John and Woodford went out into the hallway, they met the countess coming back from the terrace. When Woodford saw her, his reaction was remarkable. He stopped as if he had run into an invisible wall and stood like a man transfixed.

Olga was pulling on her gloves, but when she saw Woodford, she too gave a little gasp and froze.

John became aware of a palpable energy flowing between Olga and Woodford. They were staring at one another, their bodies so tense it seemed as if they might suddenly leap at each other – whether in anger or joy he couldn't tell. But he quickly decided that he was in the way.

"Well, I must return to my bride. We may have a war with Turkey if I don't rescue the sultan's emissary from her soon." He looked meaningfully at Woodford and added, "I trust your appointment will be fruitful."

Woodford nodded. "Perhaps you can find the lady in question and invite her to my study. I shan't be long."

John bowed. "Certainly." Then to Olga, "Countess," and was gone.

And Woodford and Olga were alone for the first time in over twenty years.

There was a long silence as they stared into each other's eyes, searching for clues about the feelings lurking in them.

Finally Olga broke the deadlock and began walking out onto the terrace. "Well, Alfred. I had hoped we could be alone tonight, at least for a moment. Why have you not called me? I've been on the island for days."

Woodford followed her, searching for the right words. "When I first heard that you were coming, I admit I was... tempted... but then I learned of your liaison with Anzilotti."

The countess laughed dismissively. "He is just a little toy." Seeing that they were alone on the terrace, she turned to him, raised her gloved hand, and caressed his cheek. "He's not a real man, like you...."

Woodford struggled to resist her. He was having trouble breathing. "Olya, it's been so many years. There is so much to say."

Hearing him use her pet name thrilled Olga and brought so many tender feelings flooding back, but a moment later his voice grew stern. "Sadly, just now I have an urgent duty to perform."

"Yes," she said, "always your duty." She ran her hand up into his hair, the hair he carefully colored in secret to strike a balance between its actual silver and his more youthful chestnut, and said, "Oh, my darling Alfy! You seem never to grow old.... How do you do that? Do you have a painting of yourself upstairs like your dear Mr. Oscar Wilde?"

Woodford took her hand in his. "My dearest Olya, you flatter me. It is you who never grows old, either in looks or spirit."

The countess moved against him. They both reacted to the memory of the way their bodies fit together so perfectly. Olga sighed, "That wonderful winter in Moscow. Why did you leave me?"

The pain of the memory struck Woodford like a knife in his heart. "It was the most difficult thing I've ever had to do, dearest Olya. But you know I was called to India, and I had to do my duty. Besides, you had your career, which I have followed from afar all these years. And I had mine, which has swept me from India, half-way around the world, and finally to this island. So many times I thought to contact you, but your lovers, your husbands— But when the Count died, I knew I had to risk it and invite you tonight." He went on with a touch of bitterness. "I had hoped you would come alone, but that was not to be." He took a breath, his eyes moist. "You see, I have never married; there could have been no one else after you."

The countess nodded sadly. "Yes. And though you know I have been with many men, in my heart, they have all been you...."

She raised herself slightly and in an instant they were kissing, tentatively at first, then passionately. Woodford could feel his heart pounding and the blood coursing through him as it had not for many years. Olga whimpered.

By a mighty exertion of will, Woodford broke away. "Once again, my duty intervenes, and I must break my heart by leaving you. But I promise, we will speak again later, in private."

The countess looked up at him, her eyes wet. "Yes, we must, please. And soon. After the next course."

Woodford bowed and said, "Until then!" He hurried toward his study as the countess rushed breathlessly back toward the dining room.

* * *

John found Burstner still lurking in the hallway. She turned to him eagerly as he approached.

"You delivered my note?"

"Yes," he answered and took her firmly by the arm. "He is most eager to see you, but first, we need to talk in private."

Burstner was startled, but composed herself. She wondered what the handsome American might want. Smiling, she said, "As you wish."

John led her through the nearest door, which opened into the trophy room. "No one will bother us in here," John said as he closed the door behind them.

The fire in the large stone fireplace threw flickering light on the rows of mounted heads of bear, caribou, mountain goats, lions, tigers and other game shot by Woodford and his predecessors. Burstner shivered, imagining her own head looking down from the wall with glass eyes.

John spoke tersely. "Fraulein, there's not much time, so let's not beat around the bush."

Burstner tried to smile seductively, but the result was only lascivious. "But Lieutenant, I do love a little beating around the bush."

John was having none of it. "You know what I mean! I'm talking about the fact that you are presently acting as an agent of the Turkish government."

In spite of herself, Burstner was momentarily stunned. She stared at him. Who was this seemingly innocuous young American that he should know so much? Perhaps, she thought, he is bluffing, just on a fishing expedition. In an amused tone, she said, "I am? What a novel idea.... and here I thought I was a German reporter."

John recited quickly from memory: "Burstner, Hildegard; born Hamburg, 1876, educated in Leipzig, graduated *cum laude*, had affair with Otto Schmidt, President of Dueling Society, who later recruited her for German Intelligence and arranged her post as foreign correspondent for *Der Geist*; in 1902 spent holidays with actress, later Countess, Olga Petrova in Finland, had brief lesbian affair. In 1909, had affair with the Turkish envoy Asaad Kelada, a notorious sado-masochist, who turned her into a double agent for the Turks." He paused for his recitation to sink in. Burstner staggered against a chair, holding herself upright. John went on, "These are only a few highlights of your really remarkable career. Shall I go on?"

Burstner managed to say, "You are very well informed."

John smiled. "Your file at the Military Information Committee is required reading for all new agents; you are quite a star. Under other circumstances, I would be thrilled to meet you in the flesh."

Burstner caught her breath and sat on the huge leather sofa, smiling crookedly. "That is gratifying, though notoriety is no advantage in our business. Fortunately, the British do not yet seem to be among my admirers.... Or am I mistaken? Is Governor Woodford as well informed as you seem to be?"

John sat beside her. "No, you are so far a closely guarded secret which we have not shared with the British, nor will we, if you agree to a very simple and lucrative proposal."

"And what is that?"

"That you work for *us*, of course."

Burstner almost laughed out loud. "Become a *triple* agent?" The idea of it was so preposterous that she found it appealing.

John saw his opening and pressed her. "Yes. You would be our pipeline into both German and Turkish intelligence."

"Really, that would be quite a fascinating challenge." She turned to him. "But extremely dangerous."

John knew he had her. He rose and approached her. "Needless to say, you would be very valuable to us." He removed a fat envelope from his uniform pocket and held it out to her. "Consider this only a down payment."

Burstner took the envelope and peeled back the flap. Peering inside, she made out a number of thousand-dollar bills. Expertly, she fanned the packet with her thumb. "Ten thousand. That is indeed a handsome sum." She closed the envelope. "And what would my first assignment be?"

John leaned in and spoke into her ear. "Woodford is carrying a secret document which the British hope might avert war. The United States government wants to know exactly what it contains. This information could be used to strengthen our position in Europe. But of course, America must not be seen to be interfering. If you can discover the contents without disrupting its delivery, you will be paid twice again as much."

Burstner was thinking it through. How perfectly this fit into her plans! With no additional risk, this would double her profits! Truly, the gods were smiling on her tonight.

After only a momentary pause, she slipped the envelope into the inside jacket pocket of her tuxedo and patted it affectionately. "This is a most interesting proposal, Lieutenant. I think I shall accept."

"Good," John said. "And now, Governor Woodford is waiting for you in his study next door."

Burstner smiled. "How convenient."

* * *

A heavily loaded cart pulled by a sway-backed mule groaned as it bumped across the paving stones of the plaza. On the seat was an ancient farmer. He pulled on the reins and the cart shuddered to a stop. Streisel ground out his cigarette and stepped out of the shadows of the portico, looking up at the dilapidated cart. The farmer whispered apologetically, "I have a load of firewood for the embassy kitchens. We will attract no notice."

Streisel nodded and pulled himself up onto the seat beside the farmer, drawing a rustic blanket over his leather greatcoat.

9. The King's Lamb

Woodford couldn't be still. He paced up and down the carpet in his study, stopping only to refill his glass with whiskey. His thoughts whirled, torn between concern over the treaty and his renewed passion for the countess. He had thought of her constantly over the years, true, but he wasn't prepared for the thrill of actually seeing, holding, kissing her.

The memory of her body against his on the terrace brought a flood of other, more explicit memories of their torrid months together that winter in Moscow, when he was a dashing young officer with a promising future, and she was the exciting young actress in Stanislavski's company. In the years since, they had each separately realized their dreams, but without her at his side, Woodford felt that the years were empty. He wondered if she felt the same way.

There was a sharp knock at the door. Woodford set down his drink and hurried to open it. There stood Burstner at last.

She looked past him into the room, checking to see if he was alone. "Governor Woodford. I hope I am not intruding? That nice American lieutenant told me you would be here."

Woodford stood aside and gestured her into the room. "Not at all, Fraulein, I've been expecting you. Please come in."

She stepped past him, moving cautiously. He tried to put her at ease. "May I offer you a drink?"

Burstner scanned the room, then turned to him. "Have you any Schnapps?"

"No," he said, "just whiskey and some cognac, I'm afraid."

Burstner grimaced. "You British and your whiskey. I'll have some cognac." She sat in one of the chairs beside the fireplace, in which a small fire was burning. Woodford moved to the sideboard and poured her the brandy, and refreshed his own glass with whiskey.

"So, what do you think about this dreadful assassination at Sarajevo?" he asked, wanting to give her an opening that would lead to what he hoped was the business at hand.

Burstner sipped the cognac. "Everyone knows the Serbs were behind it." Burstner was thinking, Look at him sweat! I'll just let him stew in his own juices for a time.

Woodford sat in the other chair, facing her, every inch the diplomat. He said, "Official Serbian involvement has not been proven. On the contrary—"

Burstner snorted. "Bah! The Serbs have harbored and supported terrorists for years! It is a danger to all of Europe. Austria will finally attack, as well they should!"

Woodford chose his next words with care: "But what if war could still be averted?"

"Impossible!"

"But the British Foreign Office hopes—"

"You British are good at hoping. But hope will not stop the war."

Woodford, out of patience, decided to force the issue. "Fraulein, you asked to see me. What is your business? Is there something you expect to receive from me?"

Burstner looked at him craftily. "Perhaps, yes."

Woodford waited for her to say more, but she just sat there, sipping her brandy. When he could stand it no longer, he blurted out, "A document of great importance?"

Burstner set her glass down and sat back in her chair, enjoying Woodford's discomfort. "Yes, several documents in fact. And of very great importance to you and our dear countess, I would think."

This brought Woodford up short. What in the world could she be talking about? How could this involve Olya? "I'm sorry, I don't understand…. The countess?"

Burstner smiled. "Yes. Doesn't she look wonderful after all these years? Almost as wonderful as that winter in Moscow…."

Sensing danger, Woodford peered at her. "You knew her then?"

Burstner got up and opened her jacket, just enough for Woodford to see the packet of letters protruding from her inside pocket. "Oh, yes. She wrote me often about you... and of course, she came to stay with me in Finland that summer when the child was born...."

Woodford was knocked back into his chair as by a physical blow. For a moment he couldn't breathe. "Child? She had a child?"

Burstner was behind his chair. She thought, Just as she said, she kept it secret from him; now I have him. Aloud, she spoke softly into his ear. "Oh, yes. You didn't know?"

"No," Woodford stammered. "I knew only that she was ill, or so she said, and had gone to Finland to recuperate, but I had no idea...."

"Yes. A daughter, a darling little daughter. Put up for adoption, of course. And these letters.... they tell the whole sad tale. They still make interesting reading."

She walked around in front of his chair and looked down at him, his fingers gripping the arms of the chair. Now for the *coup de grace,* she thought. Aloud, she said, "I have sometimes thought of publishing them...."

Woodford's face reddened. "That would be terrible! Surely, you would not...."

Burstner picked up her cognac and strolled back to Woodford's desk. "It's just a thought. If I ever needed help...."

Woodford got unsteadily to his feet. "I am not a rich man, but of course, whatever reasonable sum—"

"Ten thousand," she said without hesitation.

Woodford blanched. "Impossible! I have at most a few thousand, perhaps three at most. I offer it all, but there is no more!"

Burstner waved him into silence. She knew Woodford's means were limited, but she hadn't know how severely. Well, it was no matter. The twenty thousand from the Americans for the contents of the treaty was more than she had hoped for anyway.

She turned to Woodford. "Relax, I am not interested in your money. The kind of help I need takes the form of information."

Woodford drew himself up. "Information? What sort of information?"

"As a member of the government, I expect that you are privy to certain plans— negotiations—treaties, even?"

"No!" Woodford burst out, his hand finding the medal at his throat. "Now I see where this is going! Never will I betray my trust! Do what you will with those damn letters. I don't care what you do to me!"

Burstner leaned toward him, her face twisted. "And the countess? Do you care so little what happens to her?"

Woodford drew himself to his full height. "Where the security of His Majesty's Government is concerned, the fate of any one person is insignificant!" He stalked over to the door and threw it open. "Now I'll thank you to get out!"

Burstner was quite willing to leave. This, after all, was only a temporary setback. She was sure the countess would succeed in moving Woodford. Getting a look at the treaty would be more difficult, but an opportunity might yet present itself. And even if it did not, the American's ten thousand dollars was still safely in her pocket.

* * *

Behind the stage, well out of earshot of the chattering guests, Lydia and Nicky were arguing in fierce whispers. Nicky had grown nervous. The dinner was taking longer than planned. He felt that it was necessary to advance the timetable. "We must strike soon! Something might go wrong, and if we lose the element of surprise, all will be lost!"

Lydia took firm hold of his arm. "Nicky! Get hold of yourself! We're going to be fine! Listen to me. I've done this before, more times than you might guess, and there's not a spot on my record. You know why? Because I make careful plans and then stick to them no matter what. It's taken a year of sleeping with stuffed shirts and playing for their stupid parties to set this up, and I'm not going to risk it all because you get nervous!"

Her words, and even more her tone, stung Nicky. He looked at her as if he were seeing her for the first time, a mixture of shame and anger rising in his throat. "What a fool I have been! You don't really care about me, or my cause, do you? That sweet talk on the mountain, the lovemaking. I was just another pawn in your plan, wasn't I? You have played me like your harpsichord."

Lydia softened. "Don't be stupid, Nicky. I do care, more than I should. But whatever our personal feelings, we can't let them interfere with our plan. Now let's get back to work!"

"Yes, as you say," Nicky said, backing away from her. "I have my duty."

* * *

Upset by the interview with Burstner, Woodford needed a moment to recover and to relieve himself before going back to the dining room for the rest of the entreés. The men's toilet was thankfully empty. He rested his head against the marble wall of the urinal and breathed deeply. As he turned to button his pants, the door opened and Mustafa Ataturk stormed in.

"Ah, Governor Woodford. I have been trying to get a private word with you all night."

"Well, you have me at your disposal now, sir. I trust your conversation with Mrs. Benton was not too taxing?"

"Damn you for inflicting her on me!" Ataturk was genuinely upset. "I have never heard such rubbish about my own country before! Where do these Americans get their ideas?"

"Surely this is not what you wanted to see me about?"

"No," Ataturk said, glancing under the stall doors to make certain that they were alone. "I think you know that not everyone in the sultan's government was happy about this annexation of Cyprus by you English? Several of us have private reservations."

"Of course, I knew there was opposition to the idea. But we have proven to be a valuable and loyal ally over the past thirteen years, have we not? And you must admit, the deal is a lucrative one for Turkey."

Ataturk laughed ruefully. "For the sultan, but not for Turkey. Britain has raped the island of its resources, and your naval base is essential to your defense in this region. If the sultan were not so eager to line his pockets with your tribute, he would have seen that an even more lucrative and advantageous deal could have been made with Germany."

Woodford said, "It's too late for second thoughts now, Ataturk. The treaty has been signed, and the payment of the tribute tomorrow will seal the bargain."

"Assuming that all goes as planned. I hope for your sake nothing goes wrong, governor. I must warn you that the slightest

irregularity will give me and those who share my view the opportunity to declare the treaty null and void."

Woodford straightened his clothes. "The sultan would never
go along with that, I'm afraid."

"No?" Ataturk smiled. "I have already put before His Serene
Highness an offer from Germany that makes yours look like an
insult. He is as eager as I to see this foolish arrangement with
England abrogated."

Woodford stiffened. "My government would view such an
act as requiring the harshest of responses."

Ataturk spun on his heel, reached for the door and said, "Our
German friends are ready and willing to come to our aid if that
were to happen." He turned in the doorway. "But it is no matter. I
expect you will all be at war within weeks in any event."

* * *

Woodford had selected one of his favorite cold meat dishes
as the second *entreé*. It was a boned back of baby lamb named in
honor of his beloved King Edward VII. Edward had come to the
throne in 1901 after the passing of his mother, Queen Victoria,
and Woodford felt a tremendous affinity for the sportsman king,
who was something of a rogue – a playboy named in several di-
vorce cases – of whom Victoria had always disapproved and had
excluded from affairs of state. But once he was king, Edward had
restored vigor and dazzle to the throne, and had supported military reform. He was widely mourned when just four years ago he
had died and had been succeeded by his second son, the present
King George – also a good man, a navy man, but lacking, Woodford thought privately, the panâche of his father.

Like its namesake, the lamb was excessive, complex, and
vigorous, despite being served cold.

Selle d'Agneau de Lait Edouard VII – Lamb Edward VII

*Completely bone the rack of milk-fed baby lamb from under-
neath in such a way as to leave the skin intact; season it inside,*

> *and place in the middle a fine foie gras, studded with truffles and marinated in Marsala.*
>
> *Reconstruct the rack, and wrap it tightly in a piece of muslin; put it in a sauce pan just large enough to hold it, on a layer of pieces of bacon rind, cleared of all fat and blanched. Moisten, enough to cover, with the braising liquor of a rump of veal; add the Marsala used in marinating the foie gras, and roast for about forty-five minutes.*
>
> *Before taking out the rack, make sure that the foie gras is sufficiently cooked. Remove the muslin, and put the rack on an oval platter. Strain the cooking liquor over it, without clearing the former of fat, and set it to cool.*
>
> *When the rack is quite cold, carefully clear away the fat that is on top, first by a spoon and then by means of boiling water. Serve it cold just as it stands.*

Makarios had applauded the choice of the cold meat. It could be prepared well in advance, and so conserved the embassy's limited oven space for the hot roast, the Talleyrand of Beef, that would be the *relevé*. The cold lamb had a further advantage; it would be perfect for the main course of the dinner to be served to the small platoon of British soldiers garrisoned to the embassy.

The dinner served to the British soldiers was actually a crucial part of the plan that Nicky had developed with Lydia and Father Demetrius. Nicky had suggested to Woodford that after the British troops had patrolled the grounds before the banquet and as the guests were arriving, they would badly need a dinner break before they would have to guard the tribute all night and through the morning until the noon ceremony the following day, when the tribute itself would be turned over to the Turkish soldiers scheduled to arrive from the mainland in the morning. Since the grounds would be quiet during the dinner itself, with no one coming or going, Nicky proposed that this was when the British soldiers could enjoy a late supper. The Cypriot house guard could relieve the British troops during their dinner. And, Nicky had added, the Cypriot guards, usually a merely ceremonial group that did not carry real firearms, might even be armed during this time given the importance of the occasion.

Nicky had successfully persuaded Woodford; even Sergeant-Major Bledsoe, the senior British noncommissioned officer in command of the small garrison, had welcomed the idea.

And so now, as the lamb was being served to the guests inside, the British soldiers were in their barracks off to the side of the garden, thoroughly enjoying this welcome departure from their army rations. They were not aware that the Cypriot house guards, instead of guarding the guests or the tribute, had instead formed a ring around the barracks, ready to seal it off.

Nor did the British soldiers notice that the ration of wine they had been served to accompany the lamb had been laced with *hemlock duem*, an island herb that would ensure that they were well asleep by the end of their meal.

* * *

The lights of the embassy could be seen at the top of the hill. The cart lurched to a stop and Streisel slid silently down from the back. A brief signal and the cart continued on its way with its load of extra firewood for the embassy ovens.

Streisel moved quietly through the scrub that covered the slope and began to circle upward. As he approached a shallow ravine, his long practice in tracking alerted him to tell-tale signs of recent movement. Soon he heard snatches of whispered conversations and smelled the faint smoke of cigarettes.

He swung above the ravine and peered silently down upon a group of partisans huddled below, clutching their makeshift weapons. At their head was a priest. He was holding his beads, saying a silent rosary as a blessing over the motley group.

Streisel thought, You poor devils, a well-trained patrol would wipe you out in a minute.

But this local squabble was none of his affair. He only hoped it would not interfere with the exchange of the document. After that, he could only wish these poor fools well in their attack on the British, who would, after all, soon be enemies of the Fatherland.

Leaving the partisans to their fate, he continued up the hill the short distance to the garden wall of the embassy. A quick jump and roll and he was inside. Streisel pulled his pocket watch from beneath his long leather coat. By a shaft of light coming from the terrace above, he could see that it was not yet eleven. Still plenty of time. He moved toward the maze, which his instructions told him was at the rear of the garden.

FIFTH COURSE: THE RELEVÉ

10.   Talleyrand's Stuffed Beef

As Stefano rang the chimes for the main course, Woodford and John were standing at the top of the stairs leading into the dining room. They surveyed the scene below. The guests, blissfully unaware of the drama being played out around them, were chatting as the waiters finished clearing the entrée, and the stewards began pouring the robust Chambertin Clos de Beze 1874 that would accompany the roast meat.

"So," John said quietly, "Burstner isn't the Austrian courier?"

Woodford answered ruefully, "No, I'm afraid not. Would that she were!"

Across the room, Lydia was playing a piece by Scarlatti. When she saw Woodford and John, she looked up and smiled, nodding her head in their direction. John gave her a small wave.

Behind them, a desperate voice called out, "Alfy, help me!"

They turned to see the countess staggering toward them, coming from the powder room. Woodford rushed to her and caught hold of her arm, steadying her. "Olya! What is it? You look terrible!"

She said breathlessly, "Alfred! You must help me."

Woodford put a protective arm around her. "Let's get you some fresh air in the garden." He turned to John. "Lieutenant, would you make my excuses, please?"

"Certainly," John answered. "You can count on me."

Woodford led the countess toward the door. "Come, my dear.... The fresh air will do you good."

The countess murmured, "You were always so kind... always so kind...."

* * *

John took his place at the head table and said, "Governor Woodford regrets that he has been unavoidably detained. Some problem in the kitchen. He will be with us soon."

John then signaled Nicky to begin the service. Lydia provided a fanfare as the waiters burst into the ballroom in a grand procession. Two by two, they carried on their shoulders elaborate platforms festooned with garnishes on which sat the dish that Woodford considered the greatest beef dish ever created, Fillet of Beef Talleyrand. Napoleon's notorious foreign minister had used food as a weapon of diplomacy, and considered the chef who traveled everywhere with him to be indispensable to the success of any negotiation. The audacious Talleyrand, however, had eventually alienated Napoleon by becoming a voice of caution and conciliation, and it was for this reason that Woodford considered the choice of his most famous dish as a fitting, if rueful, commentary on the current state of international affairs.

Filet de Boeuf Talleyrand – Beef Talleyrand

Cut up the necessary number of raw truffles or mushrooms for the garnishing of each fillet. The pieces should be one inch long and 1/4 inch wide, and so pointed as to enable them to be easily stuck into the meat. Make small incisions in the fillets, and in these set the bits of truffle or mushrooms. Marinate the fillet for three hours in Madeira; wrap it in slices of bacon; tie it, and set it on the stove to braise with its marinade. When the beef is properly braised, remove the slices of bacon. Glaze the beef and set it on a plank.

Send the following garnish separately: poached macaroni, cut into pieces 1 1/2 inches long, and combined per pound with three ounces of grated Gruyere and Parmesan cheese, 1 1/2 ounces of butter, three ounces of a julienne of truffles, and three ounces of cooked foie gras cut into large dices. As an accompaniment, send a Perigueux sauce with a fine julienne of truffles or mushrooms.

The meats were accompanied by great platters of vegetables: *riz a la Greque, asperges vertes* in butter, potato croquettes, and the delicate and demanding *soufflé* of spinach with truffles. The *soufflé* had again strained Makarios and his cooks almost to the breaking point.

Nicky had helped spur on the kitchen staff. "The dinner must proceed well," he prodded the cooks. "We must lull everyone into complacency, then we will strike!" The cooks had risen to fulfill their patriotic duty, and Nicky looked out from the butler's pantry with satisfaction and mounting anticipation. The diners reveled in the extraordinary complexity and richness of the roast. Case upon case of the superb forty-year-old Chambertin was consumed, and everyone was suffused with a warm glow of satisfaction. Not one person imagined that they were in any danger, and a happier group of potential hostages could scarcely be imagined.

* * *

Burstner, who ate no red meat, had waved away the beef and now was making her way out of the dining room, intent on a cigar. She stepped onto the terrace and moved to the stairs leading down into the garden. At the bottom, she lit one of her precious *Flor Fonsecas*, made especially for her by that dear man Francisco in Havana. She inhaled deeply, letting the smoke trickle out through her nostrils. Not everything had gone right tonight, but enough – and so many possibilities remained to be explored that she was confident the outcome of this trip would justify the horrors of the sea crossings.

"Fraulein Burstner," a voice said behind her. Burstner turned and looked with surprise at the speaker, who said, "I have a proposition that I think will interest you."

Burstner smiled. "It has been a night of interesting propositions. Let's go and find someplace private."

* * *

The scent of night jasmine was strong in the garden, the moon high. Under other circumstances, it would have been an ideal night for a romantic tryst.

Woodford supported the desperate countess as they moved through the intricate maze of tall boxwood hedges, until they reached the clearing at its center. There a stone bench sat beneath an ancient statue of Athena.

Woodford lowered Olga gently onto the bench and kneeled beside her. He could no longer avoid the question that had been gnawing at him ever since his meeting with Burstner. "Olya," he said gently, "is it true? You had a child?"

The countess suppressed a sob and said, "Hildy told you? Damn her!"

Woodford sat beside her and summoned up his courage. "Was it… ours? Mine?"

Olga nodded. "A girl. I never meant for you to know."

Woodford was puzzled, hurt. "But why on earth not? If I had known, of course I would have married you!"

The countess looked up at him. "Please understand. I wanted you to choose me out of love, for myself, not out of a sense of obligation."

Woodford took a moment to digest this. "Yes," he said slowly, "at the time I would not have understood that, but now that I am older.…" He looked at her, his eyes wet. "Leaving you was the greatest mistake I have ever made, Olya, one I regret every day. Obligation or not, I should have stayed."

Olga could hold back no more and leaned against him sobbing. He held her close and caressed her hair, a tear coursing down his own cheek.

He gave her his pocket handkerchief and asked softly, "What became of the child?"

The countess took a breath, dabbing at her eyes. "A foundling home. She was such a lovely little girl…. It broke my heart, but there was no way I, a single actress, could keep her. The only thing I had to leave to her was that cameo you gave me…."

Woodford remembered. "It was the face of Athena. It reminded me of you." He looked up at the ancient statue of Athena that loomed above them, guarding the center of the maze. "And we find ourselves now, in the autumn of our lives, under her protection. How ironic."

"No," Olga said, her voice breaking, "how beautiful." And again, they kissed, this time a long, gentle kiss full of remembrance and loss.

Woodford looked into her eyes. "The girl, our daughter, she...." His voice broke as he said the words.

Olga put her hand on his cheek. "I searched for her, for years, but the records had been sealed, there was no trace." She turned away, unable to meet his gaze. "And now... my fortune is gone, my career in a shambles... and I am in such trouble...."

Woodford held her, summoning strength. "Olya, you must let me help you. Tell me what sort of trouble you are in; together we can surely work something out."

Overcome by shame, Olga got up and moved away to the edge of the clearing, one hand against the statue for support. "Oh, Alfy, I need money. So much money. And I need it at once. To-night."

Woodford got up and went to her. "How much? I have some meager savings...."

Olga turned to him. Adding together her debt to Vittorio and Burstner's demand for the letters, she forced out the words, "Fifteen thousand pounds."

Woodford was stunned. "What? I don't have nearly that much."

Olga was becoming desperate again. "But you do! You have much more!"

Woodford stared at her, uncomprehending. "What?"

At last she blurted it out. "The sultan's Tribute! You said it was worth 100,000 pounds. Who would miss a few stones?"

Woodford was rocked back on his heels. "Do you realize what you are suggesting?"

"It is a matter of life or death...."

Woodford turned away, stricken. It was again the collision of duty and love he had confronted twenty-five years before in Moscow. He regretted the choice he had made then, but now... he wasn't an impulsive junior officer any more. He knew what his choice must be.

He turned to the countess, drawing himself up to his full height. "It is unthinkable, Olya. The sultan is looking for an excuse to cancel the treaty and pass the island to Germany. The tribute *must* be paid; any irregularity would be disastrous for the British and Allied cause."

The countess was again in the throes of her hunger for the drug. Spasms of withdrawal ravaged her whole being. She begged, "We could make it look like an accident, or a burglary. No one would blame you."

Woodford was astounded. "Olga! I can't believe I'm hearing this from you!"

The countess was growing hysterical. "Don't you see that I am desperate?" She threw her arms around his neck and began kissing him. "I would do anything, anything you asked!"

Woodford pushed her away. "It is a matter of duty and honor."

Olga hissed, "Damn your duty and honor! I must have the money tonight!"

He stared at her incredulously. "What has that swine Anzilotti done to you? My poor Olya. I would make any sacrifice, but more is at stake than my reputation." Woodford drew himself up. "I will not betray my trust. There is nothing more to say."

The countess softened and looked up at him, tears in her eyes. "I'm sorry. Can I ever be forgiven?"

Devastated, Woodford could say only, "That is up to a higher power than mine."

Then he rallied himself and swore an oath: "I will punish that swine Anzilotti if it's the last thing I do!"

⋆ ⋆ ⋆

Woodford came roaring up from the garden maze with a frantic countess close on his heels. John was just returning to the dining room when Anzilotti, puzzled by the countess' prolonged disappearance, passed him in the hall on his way outside to look for her. John followed, and all four of them arrived on the terrace simultaneously.

When Woodford saw the hapless Anzilotti come through the French doors, he visibly swelled and bellowed, "Anzilotti!"

"Alfred, please!" Olga cried. "You will ruin everything!"

Vittorio shrank back. "Ah, Governor Woodford, what a splendid repast. Your chef has outdone himself—"

Woodford already had him by the lapels, nearly lifting him off his feet. "I want to speak to you in private. Come to my study at once!"

Woodford dropped Vittorio, who managed to stay upright. "If you wish," he managed.

Woodford stormed off. "At once!"

Vittorio straightened his jacket and flashed a sickly smile at the others. "You think he might be upset?" He looked to the countess. "Nothing that could interfere with our wonderful evening, or the payment of our debt of gratitude, countess?"

The countess was genuinely contrite. "I have nothing for you. I tried, but to no avail. And now, as you see, he knows our secret. I am powerless to stop him now...."

Vittorio shrunk an inch or two, then said philosophically, "Oh well, I may have other plans anyway." He turned to go and gave them a gallant bow. "*Arriverderci*! We who are about to die, salute you!"

The countess staggered and was on the verge of swooning. John caught her, "Countess, let me help you. Come, you can rest in the library."

* * *

In the garden, Streisel had moved stealthily to the entrance of the boxwood hedge maze that covered the rear of the garden at the crest of the hill that ran down to the town. It was at the center of this maze that his instructions told him to receive the document, though they did not say who might deliver it.

He had been about to enter the maze when Woodford and the countess came rushing out, obviously very upset. Streisel quickly hid behind a shrub as they passed.

When they were safely gone, he entered and found his way to the center. There he sat on the small bench beneath the statue of Athena and again settled down to wait. The waiting, he thought, was the hardest part of any mission, but the enormous stakes made it almost unbearable tonight.

SIXTH COURSE: THE SALAD

11. Russian Salad

The hallway clock was chiming eleven as the salad, placed in the French manner after the main course to lighten the palate, was served. Ironically, Woodford had selected this course as yet a third tribute to the countess.

Salade Russe – Russian Salad

Take equal quantities of carrots, potatoes, string beans, peas, truffles, capers, gherkins, sliced and cooked mushrooms, lobster meat, and lean ham – all cut into juliennes, and add a few anchovy fillets. Make a good mayonnaise sauce and mix all the ingredients, reserving some of each for garnish. Arrange it all on platters and decorate with some of the ingredients, together with some juliennes of beets and pockets of caviar.

Given what was happening to Woodford, the lush Russian salad would have turned bitter in his mouth had he tasted it. But he didn't. Woodford, like most of the other principal actors in the drama, was conspicuously absent from the table during the salad. The ballroom buzzed with speculation about the governor's strange behavior during the latter part of the evening. He was widely respected as a pillar of the empire and a paragon of good manners, and his lateness to table at several courses, and now his complete failure to reappear after the main course, was noted with considerable curiosity.

Less surprising was the absence of the countess, Anzilotti, Lydia, and Burstner. After all, odd behavior was expected from an actress, a poet, a musician, and an international journalist. The young American consul and his wife had gone missing as well, though now that gauche woman from Kansas had returned alone to the head table and was trying without much success to entertain the sultan's emissary and the other dignitaries.

Soon, however, Lydia hurriedly resumed her place at the harpsichord and played enthusiastically, hoping to fill the void caused by the absence of so many notables.

* * *

Four of the other missing characters were at that moment playing out intense confrontations, Woodford and Vittorio in the governor's study, and John and Olga next door in the library.

Vittorio opened the door to the study and found Woodford throwing down a sizable glass of whiskey. Putting on a brave face, he asked, "What was it you wished to discuss with me, governor?"

Woodford poured himself another glass and said, "I don't want to discuss anything with you, Anzilotti!"

Next door in the library, John had helped the countess to a seat and was now kneeling beside her, speaking earnestly. "Countess, I've got to talk straight to you; there isn't much time. You must not press your demands with Governor Woodford!"

The countess turned away and tried to hide her surprise; how could the American know? Had Alfred confided in this stranger?

Woodford came so close to Anzilotti that Vittorio could smell the whiskey on his breath. In a low, threatening tone, more frightening than a bellow, Woodford said, "I know what you have done to the countess, and why she owes you so much money. You will forgive her debt, and leave her, and this island, forever. I will do what I can to help her put her life back in order once you are out of it for good!"

John moved closer to the countess. "I know about your involvement in the Bolshevik party, countess, and I fear they may have put you up to this."

Olga looked at him, aghast, and said, "But why would they do that?"

Woodford fortified himself with whiskey yet again. Vittorio was surprisingly calm. "My dear Lord Woodford," he said quietly, "you could deport me, yes, but your continuation in your post here would be highly unlikely if I were to reveal your little operation...."

John went on, "If you are successful in blackmailing Woodford and thereby disrupting payment of the sultan's tribute, it would destroy the treaty between Britain and Turkey. Although an alternative deal with Germany is already in place, Russia will try to move in first. The island will be of tremendous strategic importance if there is war."

Woodford blustered, "What on earth do you mean, Anzilotti? What operation?" Vittorio helped himself to a glass of Woodford's whiskey. Woodford could only fume while he watched the Italian take a sip.

The countess shook her head. "No, it has nothing to do with Russia," she said. "Did you know, Lieutenant, that Alfred and I were once to be married? But he had to leave me, and I was devastated." In spite of himself, John was touched by the profound sadness he saw in the countess. "He never knew," she said, "but there was a child...."

Nodding appreciatively as he sipped the whiskey, Vittorio turned and said, "Why, your art smuggling and drug running, of course."

Woodford was perfectly still for a moment, the blood drained from his face, the breath knocked out of him by the sheer audacity of it. Then he managed to say, "Art smuggling? Drug running? Impossible!"

John gave the countess his handkerchief and put a supportive arm around her heaving shoulders. Gently, he said, "The governor's feelings for you are obviously still strong."

Between sobs, the countess said, "And mine for him are stronger than I expected."

"Oh, yes," Vittorio said, refilling his glass with Woodford's twenty-five-year-old, single malt whiskey, "I can prove it!"

John asked, "What about Anzilotti? What are your feelings for him?"

The countess threw back her head in disdain. "Vittorio is a monster! He introduced me to an insidious habit before which I am now powerless."

John's eyes widened. "You mean—"

Vittorio went on, "Your chef receives containers filled with vegetables and supplies from the mainland. They have false bottoms that contain large quantities of—"

In their separate rooms, John and Vittorio said the word simultaneously: "Cocaine!"

The countess nodded sadly. "Yes, cocaine. And now I owe Vittorio a fortune. And I cannot stop...."

Woodford sank into a chair as Vittorio went on. "The cocaine is then transferred to the asbestos mines. From there, it is shipped to New York hidden amidst the fibers, which no one will examine too closely. The empty vegetable containers are then returned with the false bottoms filled with black market antiquities. A highly efficient operation."

John sought out the countess's eyes and said earnestly, "For Lord Woodford's sake, and for the sake of peace, you must overcome this addiction."

Woodford was dumbfounded. Vittorio smirked, "No one would believe that you were ignorant of what was going on beneath your very nose."

The countess shook her head, "If I thought I could, there is nothing I would not do to save Alfred, but I am torn between my feelings for Alfred and the insatiable craving of every cell in my body...."

Woodford took Anzilotti by the arms. "What do you get out of all this, Anzilotti? You would risk plunging Europe into war for the paltry five thousand pounds the countess owes you?"

Vittorio held himself away from Woodford and said, "My dear Lord Woodford, I am after much bigger game. If you lose the island and control reverts to the sultan, he will in turn make a very fine arrangement with Germany, an arrangement that includes a promise that I will control *all* the drug traffic moving through Cyprus from Turkey!"

Olga drew herself up. "It will be the hardest thing I have ever done. But at least I must try! Perhaps it is not too late after all!" John helped her to her feet and she rushed from the room.

Woodford had heard enough. He drew back his arm and backhanded Anzilotti across the face, driving him to the floor in front of the fireplace. "Your plan won't work if I don't care what happens to me, will it? I would sacrifice it all: career, position, reputation, to maintain my duty to the Crown and to rescue Olga from your evil influence!" Woodford seized a large iron poker from the fireplace and lifted it over his head as Anzilotti cringed and covered his face with his arm. Taking aim at Anzilotti's head, Woodford said, "The world will be better off without you, you swine!"

The poker was descending as the door burst open and Olga rushed in, followed by John. "Alfred! Stop!" she cried, rushing to him, grabbing for his arm. "He's not worth it! I'm not worth it...."

Olga's intervention deflected the blow, and the momentum of Woodford's swing carried the poker away from Anzilotti's head and into the Italian's groin. With a terrible cry, Vittorio rolled into a ball, clutching his privates and whimpering like a baby.

Woodford dropped the poker and looked at the countess. "It's going to be all right, Olya. I won't let this rotter hurt you anymore. I'll have him arrested and deported!"

Vittorio managed to speak through his pain. "But countess, think; if I am arrested, I will have no choice but to expose the smuggling operation here in the embassy. Your dear Lord Woodford will be exposed as either a criminal or a nincompoop."

Woodford held Olga close. "What happens to me doesn't matter, Olga, not if we have each other at last. I was such a fool to leave you all those years ago, and I'll not let happiness slip through my fingers again! Together we can beat this thing that's taken hold of you!"

There was a long pause, then Olga stepped back from Woodford. She looked down at Anzilotti and spoke quietly. "I am done with you and your devil cocaine, Vittorio, I swear it!"

Woodford said, "Thank God," and pulled Anzilotti to his feet, though he was still doubled over in pain. "Come, Anzilotti, let's go see the constable!"

Vittorio looked up at Woodford with absolute malevolence. "Yes, let's! I'm sure he will be interested in examining your kitchen."

Woodford began to drag Anzilotti off as the countess blocked his way. "No!" she cried. "I cannot see you hurt, Alfred. Let him say and do what he will. He will not get what he wants from either of us, but your reputation will be saved."

Woodford hesitated, and Olga put her hands on his chest, imploring him. "Please, Alfy, I could not live knowing that I had cost you your good name."

Reluctantly, Woodford released Anzilotti, who slowly straightened up, still in pain but managing a crooked smile. "You show uncommon good sense for an Englishman, Lord Woodford."

Vittorio started for the door, but John blocked his way. "Don't think you're home free, Anzilotti. I've got my eye on you!"

Vittorio pushed past him and hobbled out. "Then be careful not to blink, Lieutenant."

John turned to Woodford. "I better watch him," he said, "and besides, we'll all be missed." Woodford nodded and John hurried after Anzilotti.

Woodford and Olga rushed into each other's arms. "We will beat this thing together," Woodford said.

Olga stiffened as a thought struck her. "Burstner... she has my letters. She can still ruin us both. We must get them back."

* * *

In the barracks, all but one of the British soldiers were sleeping peacefully. The wine laced with hemlock had done its work. Only Sergeant-Major Bledsoe, the only tee-totaller in the group, was awake. He looked fondly at his sleeping men. "It's been a hard couple of days, and a hard night yet to come," he thought. "Let them catch a few winks. It'll do them good."

* * *

The clock in the hallway was striking the half-hour as Olga and Woodford emerged from the library. They started toward the ballroom when Nicky rushed up behind them. "Your lordship," he said breathlessly, "you are needed on the terrace at once! It is urgent!"

Woodford turned apologetically to the countess, but she said, "You go ahead, Alfy, I can find my own way back."

Woodford followed an obviously terrified Nicky onto the terrace. "What is so urgent, Nicky?"

Nicky led him to the balustrade and pointed down. "See for yourself," he said. Woodford leaned over the railing and peered into the darkness. At the base of the stairs some twenty feet below, he could see several Cypriot guardsmen kneeling beside a grotesquely misshapen body.

Woodford rushed down the stairs two steps at a time, almost dislodging one of the terracotta monkeys that decorated the marble railing. The kneeling group of guardsmen rose and parted as he approached. One shone his lantern on the body, and by its beam Woodford recognized Burstner's face. Her features were frozen in an attitude of surprise. Her shirtfront and jacket were soaked with blood.

It took Woodford only a moment to regain his equilibrium. He turned to Nicky, who had rushed down after him. "Does anyone else know about this?"

"No, sir," Nicky said. "I came to find you as soon as she was discovered."

"Good," Woodford said, "let's keep it that way." He nodded toward the potting shed that occupied an alcove under the terrace and ordered the men, "Take her inside."

Once Burstner was laid on the potting table, Woodford dismissed the guardsmen. He turned to Nicky and said, "Go back inside and make sure the dinner continues exactly as before. If anyone inquires after Fraulein Burstner, say only that she was called away on urgent business for her newspaper."

Nicky nodded and left. As soon as he was sure he was alone, Woodford bent over the body and began unceremoniously to search it. He patted Burstner's jacket and pants pockets and felt nothing. Steeling himself, he tore open her bloody shirt front. Just beneath one of her wrinkled breasts, unfettered by any undergarment, was a small slit. Woodford reckoned that it was the entry wound made by a small, thin dagger. It had penetrated directly to the heart – an expert thrust, he thought. This was not the work of an amateur. He paused for only a moment, then unbuttoned her pants, looking for a concealed pocket, anything that could hold the letters.

But there was nothing. Damn, Woodford thought, wiping his bloody hands, whoever killed her must have taken them.

* * *

In the woods below, the waiting Cypriots got silently to their feet as a whispered command was passed from group to group. "Get ready!" Weapons were checked, hearts began to pound with excitement. Then all knelt as Father Demetrius whispered a benediction. "God, bless us in what we do this night. May it be the first step in the journey to the freedom for which we have so long prayed." Then his voice grew stern. "And above all, help us to remember that we will do all we can to avoid all bloodshed and mean no physical harm to anyone."

The men nodded, his message received.

Each man then made a private act of contrition, knowing that in spite of all their good intentions and planning, they might, in the next few minutes, meet their God.

* * *

Streisel rose from the bench as he heard a rustling. Someone was moving through the hedgerow and approaching his position. He stiffened and instinctively drew a revolver from beneath his leather coat.

But then a quiet voice said in impeccable German, "Ich glaube, daß wir uns hier treffen sollten, *(I believe we are to meet here.)*"

"You are early," Streisel whispered, "it is not yet midnight."

"There is no time to lose. What I have for you to relay to Minister Berchtold cannot wait. The fate of Europe depends on it."

Warily, Streisel lowered his revolver. "Yes," he said, "I will report to his Excellency tonight."

"Very well, then," the voice said, "I have it here. Come closer and let me place it in your hands."

SEVENTH COURSE: THE FLAMBÉ

12. Nero's Bombe

There was a stir in the dining room as first Vittorio, limping and stooped, and a few moments later John, rigid with anger, returned to their places. After a few more minutes, the countess returned, visibly shaken and looking years older. Helping her down the stairs was Shirley.

The diners were abuzz with the startling re-appearance of the four of them. *Sotto voce,* many began to advance various theories about it.

"Darling," Shirley said to John as she returned to the table, "I was just going into the powder room when that poor countess almost fainted. I tried to help, but she looks terrible."

"Don't worry," John said, "she'll be fine. It's none of our business, anyway." He smiled at Ataturk and the other diners, who smiled back but were as curious as everyone else.

Nicky was breathless with anticipation, beads of sweat forming on his brow; soon the flaming course, which was the signal to begin the assault, would be served, but Nicky had to wait until Woodford returned. The moments dragged on. What could possibly be keeping him this long?

Nicky glanced up at Lydia, who continued to play as beautifully as ever. She threw him a puzzled look of exasperation and he answered with a tiny shake of the head. To help fill the time, he went into the kitchen and ordered the waiters to start pouring the traditional British celebratory drink, a Claret Cup, that would accompany the flaming course.

Le Cup de Vin Rouge – Red Wine Cup
Put into a crystal bowl one ounce of sugar, the rind and three slices of one lemon, an equal quantity of orange, one strip of cu-

> *cumber peel, one tablespoon of Angostura Bitters, and two ounces each of Brandy, Maraschino, and white Curacao. Complete with one and a half bottles of good red wine and a bottle of soda. Cover and let the whole infuse. Strain, and add a few pieces of very clean ice and a few leaves of fresh mint.*

As the Claret Cup was being poured, Woodford at last came down the dining room stairs. He had stopped in the toilet to wash his hands, splash water on his face, and straighten his clothing, checking carefully for any stray spots of Burstner's blood. As he moved toward the head table, he called on every shred of his diplomatic skill, smiling and even stopping casually to chat with a few of the guests, looking impossibly composed under the circumstances.

As Woodford approached the table, John looked up expectantly, asking with his eyes if anything untoward had happened. By way of answer, Woodford shook his head slightly in the negative, then turned to the other guests at the table and made his apologies: "I'm sorry that some last-minute matters have kept me from you for so long. Please forgive me."

The guests all dismissed his concern, saying that they had been enjoying themselves famously. As Woodford sat, Mustafa Ataturk leaned toward him and, barely able to disguise the hope he felt, asked, "What was the commotion outside just now? I trust nothing has happened that will interfere with the prompt payment of the tribute tomorrow?"

Woodford said only, "It was nothing, just a guest who had too much wine." Ataturk, inwardly disappointed, made a show of nodding sympathetically.

Shirley rose and said, "I'm afraid I have to be excused again. I didn't make it to the powder room just now, and it's been a while since the intermission."

John said, "Hurry back, dear, I think the next course is almost ready."

"Promise," Shirley said and hurried away.

At the rear table, the countess was watching Woodford regain his seat across the room. She wondered why he had been so long returning, and tried to suppress the nameless fears that flooded her mind. Vittorio leaned close and gestured toward

Burstner's empty seat with a crooked smile. "If we are lucky, perhaps she won't be coming back."

Nicky came out of kitchen just as Woodford returned, and went eagerly to his side. Woodford asked, "Are we ready for the next course?"

"There was a brief delay in the preparation of the flambé, sir. It is very delicate. But now all is ready."

Woodford nodded. "Very good, Nicky. You may proceed with the service."

Nicky signaled to Lydia, who struck a triumphant chord, then rose and hurried unnoticed from the stage.

Nicky next signaled to Stefano, then moved quickly up the stairs out of the dining room and toward the study.

Stefano immediately passed the signal to Makarios at the kitchen door, who turned and signaled the sous-chef, who waved to the pastry chef at the kitchen door, who called to a cook stationed on the loading dock, who flashed a signal light to the partisan lookout at the brow of the hill behind the garden, who flashed a torch at a man on an electric power pole that carried the electric lines up the hill to the embassy. One quick snip, an arc of electricity, and everywhere in the embassy lights flickered and went out.

In the town below, the church bells began to ring.

The diners murmured in the sudden darkness. Then suddenly the kitchen doors burst open and all the waiters entered carrying large platters from which great flames rose. The audience cried out appreciatively and began to applaud the *flambé*. Perhaps it was an irony of fate that made Woodford select a flaming dish that had been inspired by the burning of Rome.

Bombe Nero – Nero's Bomb

Take a dome-mould and coat it with vanilla ice-cream with Caramel; fill it with vanilla mousse, combined with small, imitation truffles, the size of small nuts, made from chocolate.

Turn out the Bombe on a thin cushion of sweet pastry. Cover the whole with a thin layer of Italian meringue. Decorate the sides by means of a pastry bag with meringue, and set the whole

> *in the oven to glaze quickly. On taking the Bombe out of the oven, pour some hot rum into the bowl and light it when serving.*

Vittorio was impressed by the display. He said to his table-mates, "Woodford has really outdone himself. This is the most impressive presentation of a dessert I have ever seen!" He reached over to Burstner's place and slid her dessert plate toward his own, saying, "I'm sure Fraulein Burstner won't mind if I have her serving as well as my own."

* * *

In the barracks, Sergeant-Major Bledsoe heard the church bells, then bolted upright as the lights went out. Something was wrong! He tried to rouse one of his corporals and became alarmed when the man was slow to respond. Suspecting foul play, he began shaking all the men awake. "Up, lads! Something's going on! Ready arms!"

The soldiers, shaking their heads to try to clear the fog from their brains, took their rifles from the rack beside the door and stumbled out into the night. There they were amazed to see a line of Cypriot house guards surrounding their barracks, rifles leveled and ready.

Inside the barracks, Bledsoe tried to send a distress call on the military radio. The naval base at Akrotiri was several hours away, but it didn't matter; the radio was dead. He rushed outside and was brought up short by what he found: his men facing the line of Cypriot guards. He stared at the scene in disbelief, then barked to his men, "Hold your fire, lads, until we find out what's going on."

Climbing over the edge of the hill and rushing into the garden, Father Demetrius stopped short in front of the line of Cypriots. He was amazed and alarmed to see the British soldiers not only awake, but armed and ready. Determined to avoid bloodshed, the priest turned to the Cypriot guards. "No one is to shoot," he ordered them.

Bledsoe called out, "Father! What the devil is all this? What do you people want?"

"Nothing but what is rightfully ours," Father Demetrius answered. "Lay down your arms and no one will be harmed, I give you my word as a priest."

Bledsoe was flabbergasted. "I'm afraid I can't give such an order, Father. It looks like we have a Mexican stand-off here."

Then there was silence. Neither the priest nor the sergeant-major so much as blinked. On both sides, tension mounted, sweat poured down faces, fingers on triggers twitched. One of the Cypriot guards standing behind the priest, a young fourth cousin of Nicky's, began to shake violently.

"Marco!" Father Demetrius ordered. "Stand fast!" But Marco felt his head swim. He knew he was losing consciousness. As he fell, he involuntarily fired. One of the British soldiers cried out and fell.

Immediately a volley of shots rang out from both sides. "Bloody hell!" Bledsoe cried, "we're for it now. Come on, lads, we'll fight our way out."

* * *

"Bravo!" Vittorio cried, "fireworks too!" But as the frantic voices of fighting men reached them, Vittorio and the other diners began to suspect that this was not simply an elaborate display. Everyone fell silent.

Terrified by the gunshots, the waiters stood momentarily frozen, holding their platters, but a moment later Stefano cried, "We've gone too far to turn back! Do it!"

The waiters hurled the flaming platters onto the tables.

The flaming brandy spread at once throughout the ballroom. Women screamed and men began beating at the flames with their jackets. In the confusion, Makarios and the other cooks ran in from the kitchen and surrounded the diners, brandishing knives and cleavers.

From all sides, there were shots and explosions. Woodford tried to make himself heard in the chaos of the dark ballroom. "Please remain calm, everyone, stay in your places."

* * *

At that moment, in Woodford's study, Lydia and Nicky were feverishly at work. An armchair was wedged against the heavy door, holding it shut. The painting of King George and Queen Mary over the mantel had been swung aside, revealing the embassy safe. Nicky held an electric torch by which Lydia finished expertly packing the hinges with dynamite.

Lydia struck a match and lit the fuse. "Down!" she commanded.

Together they huddled behind an overturned sofa and held their hands tightly over their ears. The explosion went unnoticed in the turmoil outside.

Choking on the thick smoke, Lydia and Nicky rushed to the safe. Its door now hung askew. Lydia pulled on gloves and gingerly tugged at the hot metal.

"Give me a hand," she said to Nicky as she pulled out the metal chest, adorned with the royal coat of arms. They lifted it onto the desk. By the light of Nicky's torch, Lydia pried open the simple lock. She lifted the lid and withdrew a bag of gemstones. She hurriedly laid it on Woodford's desk and opened it.

Diamonds, rubies, sapphires, emeralds glistened in the torchlight. "Aren't they beautiful?" Lydia was in rapture. "Beautiful! A hundred times over!"

She turned smiling to Nicky and was surprised to see tears streaming down his face.

"Forgive me," he said, and swung the iron poker.

* * *

"I hate the dark! Countess, where are you?" Vittorio was under the table, grasping at her skirts, trying to pull her under. There was more gunfire outside and Vittorio became hysterical. "We are all going to be killed! I don't want to die!"

The countess pulled free of his grasp and hissed, "Shut up, you coward!" She set off into the jumble of overturned tables and chairs, swooning women and protective men, determined to find Woodford. The thought that Alfred was in danger so flooded her with adrenaline that the symptoms of her drug withdrawal abated and she rushed on, driven by courageous purpose.

* * *

The well-trained British soldiers, their minds too now cleared by adrenaline, formed a skirmish line and broke through the encircling Cypriots who, truth be told, were terrified by actual combat. Soon the British were in a defensive line beneath the terrace, blocking the way to the embassy. From the dark woods, partisan marksmen fired at them, keeping them pinned behind the garden statuary.

Father Demetrius had herded the retreating Cypriot guards back down the hillside, dragging the unconscious Marco with them. A few feet below they joined the partisans crouching beneath the brow of the hill.

"Father," one of the oldest men asked, "what will we do?"

Father Demetrius was in turmoil. This was not supposed to be happening. Their plan had been predicated on surprise and the peaceful containment of the British soldiers. But now a British soldier had been wounded, no one knew how badly, and there would be no hiding the mobilization of the *enosis* movement. This might be their last and best chance to strike a meaningful blow for years.

"Come," he called to the partisans. "The world is watching! Let us at least make a show of it!"

* * *

Staying low, Woodford scuttled through the prostrate diners as bullets continued to fly overhead. He made for the French doors, determined to see where the gunshots were coming from. Once through the doors, he ran, half-crouched, to the balustrade and peered between two of the pillars.

He could see a small group of British soldiers huddled in the garden below. Muzzle flashes lit the dark woods beyond the garden, and bullets ricocheted off the marble walls of the terrace. The soldiers were firing at the muzzle flashes in the woods, but the gunmen there were obviously moving constantly.

"Good show!" Woodford called down to his men. "Hold them as long as you can!"

Sergeant-Major Bledsoe called up to him, "I don't think we can last long, sir! There's too many of them."

"Call the naval base for reinforcements," Woodford yelled.

"No good, sir," Bledsoe cried. "I tried first thing from the barracks, but the radio failed when the electricity went out. We're on our own until the Turks come in the morning. We'll try to stop them at the crest of the hill!" Bledsoe and the other soldiers moved away to form a skirmish line.

"Damn!" Woodford said aloud to himself. "I'm not going to surrender the embassy—"

The blow caught him just behind his right ear. In the split second before unconsciousness came, he thought, "Yes, you really do see stars…"

* * *

John was creeping among the hysterical forms huddled on the ballroom floor, calling Shirley's name. He heard an answer: "Here! I'm here." He rushed in the direction from which the voice had come, under one of the few tables still upright.

John ducked under and reached for her, but when she turned to him he saw not his Shirley, but a rather homely young woman. "I beg your pardon," he said, "I was looking for a different Shirley."

"Under the circumstances," the woman said, "won't I do?"

"Lieutenant," a familiar voice called from nearby. John peered out and saw the countess scurrying on all fours toward him. He turned back to the wrong Shirley and said, "Excuse me, please," and crawled out.

"Oh, thank heaven," the countess said. "Have you seen Alfred?"

John raised his head and looked toward the terrace. A bullet crashed through one of the French doors and he ducked back down. "I think he went out there," he told the countess.

"Isn't that just like him," Olga said, "rushing straight into the thick of it." She stood up.

"What are you doing?' John exclaimed.

"I'm going to be with the man I love." She ran toward the French doors.

"Oh, Lord," John said, but gentleman that he was, he rushed after her.

The countess pushed through one of the doors that was still intact. Shots rang out and she took refuge behind the statue of Artemis.

John pushed through the door and knelt beside her. A soldier in the garden below fired a flare, and by its garish light they could momentarily make out the form of Governor Woodford lying in a heap by the balustrade.

"Alfred!" the countess cried, and mindless of the bullets that flew overhead, she rushed to him.

John was close behind. Woodford had been stripped of his jacket and cummerbund.

The countess lifted Woodford's head and cradled it in her lap. She screamed when she saw his blood on her hand. She hugged him, crying, "Alfred! Oh, my dear Alfred, you can't be dead!"

John felt for the carotid pulse in Woodford's neck. "He's alive," he told the distraught countess.

"Oh, thank God."

"Lord Woodford!" John slapped Woodford into consciousness. When Woodford opened his eyes, John asked, "What's happened? Who did this to you?"

Woodford stirred and with Olga's help raised himself up on one elbow. He stared uncomprehendingly at them for a moment, and then awareness returned. "I don't know," he said. "I was hit from behind."

Woodford moved and cried out. John examined the wound on the back of Woodford's head and said, "It's a nasty cut and bruise, but there's not much bleeding."

The countess reached down and tore a strip of brocade from her gown and pressed it against Woodford's wound.

Woodford felt the night chill against his skin. He felt for his jacket, then looked down and saw that he had been stripped; his jacket and dickey were gone, his pleated shirt torn open, his pants ripped. Worst of all, his cummerbund was gone and the document with it. Desperately, he clawed at the ground around him. Woodford's face crumpled. "The treaty! They've taken the treaty! All is lost!"

A bullet tore a piece of marble from the railing beside John's head. "We've got to get out of here," John yelled. He pulled Woodford up and put one of his arms around his shoulder. "You take the other," he told the countess.

Woodford rose painfully to his knees and threw his other arm around Olga's shoulder.

"My study," Woodford said. "I have some guns there."

* * *

Nicky knelt beside Lydia and placed his face close to hers. Thank God, he could feel her breath against his cheek. He took the bag of gems from her hands. These, he thought, will go to Father Demetrius when all this is over.

Nicky's confused emotions swirled so in his head and heart that he felt dizzy, as if he were in a dream. He knew that he was ashamed of what he had done, but he was not even sure if he had acted out of jealousy, or hurt, or the desire to make sure the revolution would have all the money it needed.

In any case, he couldn't risk carrying the gems into the chaos outside. A safe hiding place had to be found.

* * *

As John and the countess helped Woodford down the dark hall toward the study, John thought he saw Nicky running from the room.

"Nicky!" he shouted. "Help us!"

But the figure disappeared down the hall toward the front door without pausing.

They found the study door ajar and pushed their way in. In the pitch black room, the smell of cordite was so heavy that they all began coughing. Woodford said, "There's a torch in my desk." John left Woodford with Olga and fumbled to the desk. He soon found the small electric torch and shone it around the room.

The painting of the king and queen swung on its hinges, and behind it the safe gaped open.

When he saw the open safe, Woodford's wound was forgotten. He rushed to it and groped inside. His shoulders slumped and he turned slowly. "Our woes come not singly but in battalions," he said. "The sultan's tribute is gone! Utterly lost, and no time to replace it before the ceremony tomorrow. I fear the island is lost to us."

John came forward, but almost tripped on a body lying crumpled behind the desk. "Look here!" he cried. "It's Miss Seymour."

Woodford and the countess rushed over and took the torch from John as he knelt and lifted Lydia's head, feeling for a pulse. "Oh, Lord," Woodford said. "Not another!"

"Another?" the countess asked. "What do you mean, another?" Woodford looked guiltily at John and Olga. "I haven't had a chance to tell you," he said, "but Fraulein Burstner was found murdered less than an hour ago."

There was no time for shock; Lydia was stirring. "She's only been knocked out," John said. "She's got a nasty bruise and bump on her head. Give me some brandy!"

Woodford poured a glass of cognac from the Tantalus on the sideboard. He handed it down and John put it to Lydia's lips. She coughed and opened her eyes. "Who... where..?" she asked and sat up, almost swooning again. They lifted her onto the armchair beside the desk.

"You're going to be all right," John assured her. "Just a doozy of a headache."

Woodford lit the candles on the desk. "Who did this to you?" he asked.

Lydia felt her head and almost blurted out the truth, but quickly thought better of it and said instead, "I don't know... it was dark...."

The countess knelt beside her and gave her another sip of brandy. As she did, she noticed the necklace around Lydia's neck. It had come out of her dress in her fall. From the golden chain hung the cameo. The countess took it in her fingers and exclaimed, "Miss Seymour, this cameo... where did you get it?"

Lydia was still groggy. She said, "I don't know. I've just always had it... as long as I can remember."

The countess held it up to the light. The face of Athena was picked out in white against the blue background. Her fingers trembled. She asked, "Does it have an inscription on the back?"

"Why, yes," Lydia said, "how did you know?"

The countess turned the cameo over. She stared at it a moment, perfectly still. Then she looked up at Woodford and said, "It's just one word. It says, '*forever.*' That night in Moscow...."

Woodford stared, unbelieving. He too knelt and looked closely at the cameo, then looked as closely into Lydia's face. "Is it possible?' he breathed.

Lydia looked from the countess to Woodford, then back, thinking they must have gone mad. "What is it?" she asked. "You're frightening me."

The countess reached out tentatively, then tenderly, caressing Lydia's face. "Yes!" she said. "I can see it now."

Woodford nodded slowly. "Yes," he said, "I thought she looked familiar...."

Lydia demanded, "What are you talking about?"

The countess embraced her and said only, "Daughter!"

Lydia pulled back from her embrace and stared into her face. Slowly, the recognition formed. Breathlessly, Lydia said, "Mother?" The countess nodded. Lydia turned to Woodford. "Father?"

Woodford smiled, then caught Lydia as she fainted dead away.

"Put up your hands!" Makarios stood in the doorway, still in his white chef's jacket and toque, a shotgun in his hands.

Woodford jumped up and reached toward the gun rack behind the desk, but a blast from Makarios' shotgun shattered the rack and sent shards of glass and wood flying.

"Don't make me shoot you, governor," Makarios said, "though you deserve it for that damn menu you planned!"

EIGHTH COURSE: THE DESSERT

13. Sunset Ice

Outside, the gunfire slowed, then stopped. The British soldiers were still pressed against the embassy wall beneath the
grand terrace. By the moonlight, they could see the mass of Cypriots cresting the hill. Steadily, the partisans advanced, until they
reached the back edge of the garden maze. There they stopped.

In the silence, Sergeant-Major Bledsoe, himself wounded in
his right shoulder, looked out at the mass of men and older boys
wielding their makeshift weapons. "Blimey," the sergeant-major
muttered to his corporal, "it's the whole bloody town. We don't
have a prayer." He signaled his men to form a skirmish line facing the townsfolk. "No one shoots until I give the order," he
called. He was hoping that some way could still be found to
avoid a bloodbath.

The two lines faced each other in silence, separated only by
the garden maze. On the Cypriot side, Father Demetrius was also
praying that a deadly confrontation could be avoided. He gathered up his cassock and called, "Parlay!"

Bledsoe called back, "Come ahead!" Then to his men, he
cautioned, "Hold your fire, lads!"

Father Demetrius walked fearlessly into the no-man's-land
between the two groups, holding his Bible above his head with
both hands. Bledsoe came forward to meet him and the two men
faced one another.

"Well, Father," Bledsoe said, "this is a hell of a mess."

"Yes. But surely as civilized men we can find a way out. We
wish only to bring our plight to the attention of the world. Let us
end this without further bloodshed. In the name of *enosis*, I call
on you British to lay down your – "

A shot rang out. Father Demetrius staggered, clutching his
throat. He made a strangling sound, then sank to his knees and

fell forward. Unnoticed by either side, a figure in a long black leather coat, a slouch hat pulled low, had risen from the center of the maze and stood with a smoking revolver in one hand. As quickly and silently as it had appeared, it sank from sight.

Bledsoe retreated, staring in disbelief at the fallen priest.

The Cypriots too stood in shock, not knowing what to do.

The British soldiers stared at one another.

"Bloody hell," Bledsoe cried, "who fired that shot?"

"It was none of us," the corporal said. Then, seeing the Cypriots standing in disarray, he tugged at Bledsoe's sleeve and whispered, "But don't look a gift horse in the mouth."

Bledsoe nodded and called, "Advance, lads!"

The British soldiers rushed forward. The townsfolk, who had suffered only a few wounds so far, stared at the advancing line. Farmers, ranchers, and tradesmen, they had no experience in war, and this night's foray had been as much daring-do as they collectively possessed. Without the leadership of Father Demetrius, they lost their nerve. Dropping their weapons, they scrambled back down the hill and melted into the dark woods. The soldiers pursued them a bit down the hill, but Bledsoe called them back. "No use going after them, lads, they know these woods too well. We'll round them up in town tomorrow." The soldiers regrouped in the garden. The brief rebellion was over.

Three of the British soldiers had been wounded, though in the darkness and confusion no one had been mortally hit. Even Father Demetrius, though his neck wound was serious, was still alive. He and the wounded soldiers were taken into the barracks, where a makeshift aid station was set up.

"Now," Bledsoe said, "there's the problem of the people inside. Are the waiters still holding them hostage?"

* * *

Inside the embassy itself, Stefano and the waiters, armed with kitchen knives and cleavers, surrounded the guests in the ballroom. The guests cowered in corners and behind overturned tables, husbands comforting sobbing wives.

Suddenly there was a collective gasp when Chef Makarios appeared at the top of the stairs, his shotgun slung over his arm.

He turned and with a wave of his weapon ushered in Woodford, still disheveled, who supported a trembling countess, followed by John, who supported a dazed Lydia. The four of them came down the stairs and moved resolutely into the room, armed waiters shrinking back at their approach.

Then, silhouetted in the French doors leading out onto the terrace, Sergeant-Major Bledsoe appeared. Makarios raised his shotgun, but undeterred, Bledsoe stepped forward and called to him. "It's over, Makarios. Father Demetrius has been wounded, your supporters have retreated, and my soldiers have the embassy surrounded."

Makarios took in the news, then defiantly met Bledsoe's gaze. "But we have your guests."

Bledsoe looked out over the cowering diners. He turned to Woodford. "Governor? This has to be your call."

Woodford considered a moment, then turned to Makarios. "Surely we can come to some mutually satisfactory solution. I assume that with Father Demetrius out of the picture, Nicky is now your leader?"

Makarios nodded. Woodford looked around for Nicky, but he was nowhere to be seen.

Woodford looked up at Makarios and said, "I'm sure that neither the good Father nor Nicky would want any further discomfort to be visited upon our guests. It will only hurt your cause if you are seen to be a mere uncivilized rabble."

Makarios considered this. He turned to Stefano, who had joined him on the stairs, and they held a short whispered conference. "Where the hell is Nicky?" Makarios asked.

"Don't know. But what Bledsoe says is true. I looked outside. They have us surrounded."

Lydia was still standing with John nearby. She stepped forward and confronted Makarios and Stefano, saying, "Don't be stupid. Woodford is right. Treat these people right. I'm sure it is what Nicky and Father Demetrius would say if they were here."

Makarios glanced at Stefano, who appeared to agree with Lydia.

"All right," he announced to Woodford, "we will guarantee your safety. But you are still our hostages until we decide what to do with you."

Woodford turned and his gaze swept the ballroom. His guests stared expectantly back, eager for some explanation. After a deep breath, he began in a clear voice. "On behalf of His Majesty's Government, I offer my deepest apology for the inconvenience you have all suffered. I regret to say that certain elements of the local population have had the bad taste to interrupt our celebration with what the British Foreign Office would call a 'native uprising.' "

While this much was already clear to everyone, at least Woodford's official confirmation helped to quiet several rumors of impending mass slaughter. He went on. "Until such time as demands are made and negotiations undertaken, I must ask your indulgence. I assure you that no further harm will come to you."

There was a general sigh of relief and a smattering of applause throughout the dining room as everyone came out of hiding. Woodford, of course, had no such assurance and hadn't the foggiest notion of what might happen next, but he felt compelled to say what he thought his guests wanted to hear. In the meantime he was determined that decorum would be observed.

At a further signal from Makarios, some of the waiters righted the tables and some semblance of order was restored. Candles were lit and placed throughout the room.

Woodford joined John and the countess at the head table, where Ataturk and the ambassadors and their wives received them, embracing in their common travail.

"Has anyone seen my wife?" a concerned John asked. No one had.

Woodford tried to calm John's fears. "Perhaps she took refuge in the powder room when the fighting started." He turned to Makarios. "Can someone go and see?"

Makarios nodded to Stefano, who rushed away.

Woodford began moving through the dining room, asking after the condition of the guests. He was relieved to find that everyone was fine, aside from some minor burns and cuts; only their dignity had been seriously wounded.

Soon Stefano appeared at the head of the stairs holding Vittorio by the scruff of the neck. "I found him hiding in the women's toilet, sitting up on a commode so his feet wouldn't show," Stefano said with disdain.

"Bring him here!" Woodford commanded.

Stefano dropped Vittorio like a dirty rag. Olga and John rose.

"No, my friends," Woodford said, holding up a hand to them. "Leave him to me."

"Fat chance!" John said and rushed at Vittorio saying, "All right, Anzilotti, what have you done with my wife?

Vittorio reflexively cringed as John approached. "Please, Lieutenant, I'm afraid you have had too much cognac. I have not seen Mrs. Benton."

John cocked his right arm. Woodford tried to intervene. "John, please, as much as I share your feelings--" But with no hesitation John punched Vittorio on the jaw, knocking him sprawling.

"That's how we handle vermin like you back home, Anzilotti! Now where is my wife?"

Vittorio covered his head against another blow and rolled into a ball. As terrified as he was of physical pain, he was more afraid that he might wet himself. In a tremulous voice, he pleaded, "I remind you, I am an Italian national—"

Woodford scoffed, "Your government won't protect you when they learn of your filthy drug and art smuggling!"

Vittorio looked up and countered, "You should be more careful what you say in public, Governor. You have no evidence of these charges. And even if you had proof of a drug operation, I remind you that cocaine is an entirely legal substance under local and Italian law." He glanced at John, who was barely restraining himself. "And the laws of the United States, for that matter. And anyway, you are not one to throw the first stone, Governor Woodford, given the interesting episodes of your past, you and the countess here—"

Woodford had heard enough. "You! Anzilotti, you killed Burstner and took the letters! Hand them over or I'll kill you myself, I swear...."

As Woodford lunged at Vittorio, the countess cried out, "No, Alfred!"

Woodford turned. Olga was standing holding a pearl-handled derringer she had withdrawn from her handbag. She held it outstretched, her hand shaking so violently that everyone stepped back, not sure where her shot might go. The diners nearby retreated under their tables yet again. Trembling, Olga cried, "Vittorio, you will never do to another woman what you have done to me!"

Vittorio was indeed now wetting himself but was too terrified to care. He begged, "Please, countess, I swear I knew nothing of Burstner's death nor of any letters, this is the first I hear –"

As she pulled the trigger, John lunged and tried to knock the gun from her hand, but succeeded only in deflecting the shot, which struck Lydia. Lydia spun and fell. Woodford ran to her and lifted her head, but she was unconscious. Helpless and horrified, he looked up at Olga.

The countess shrunk back. She cried out, "My God, what have I done? Daughter...."

She looked down at Lydia in Woodford's arms. She still held the derringer, which had two barrels, and so contained another bullet. She raised it slowly.

"I have brought only pain to those I love. But no more! Alfred, I love you, you are the only one I have ever truly loved! Remember that!"

She raised the gun to her temple. Everyone in the room gasped, and many looked away in horror. Woodford cried out, "No, Olya!" and leapt toward her.

But it was John, standing behind the countess, who managed to wrest the gun from her hand.

John spun and pointed the gun at Makarios, who in the confusion had lowered his shotgun. "All right, you," John ordered, "tell your men to put down their weapons or I'll blast you to hell!"

There was a shot and John whirled, hit in the shoulder.

Nicky stood on the stage. He held a smoking rifle in his hand. "Drop the gun, Lieutenant," he said, "or the next one will finish you."

Woodford said, "Do as he says, John, he is an expert marksman."

Reluctantly, John dropped the derringer and kicked it away.

Nicky lowered the rifle. He came down from the stage and walked toward them. Everyone shrank back at his approach, until he stood alone in the center of the room surrounded by the anxious crowd. From his jacket he withdrew a piece of parchment tied with a ribbon and sealed with the royal seal. Holding it up, he said, "Have your petty intrigues made you forget the treaty? Here is the fate of Europe!"

Woodford reflexively moved toward Nicky, but Makarios menaced him with the shotgun. "Nicky!" Woodford cried. "It was you who knocked me out and took the treaty! Is this how you repay my trust?

Nicky scoffed, "Your *trust*? Your arrogance! All of you! The Turks, the Italians, the French, and all the rulers of empires, you sat comfortably while we served your meals, scrubbed your floors, washed your clothes. Now, I will burn all your empires down!"

Nicky moved to the nearest table. He lifted the treaty toward one of the candles there. Everyone was transfixed, staring at the flame and the treaty. No one noticed Lydia stirring.

Woodford cried, "Nicky! Don't! Think of the thousands of innocent lives that document could save!"

"What of the thousands of lives your tyranny has ruined? We are tired of being your pawns. Now we will watch as you destroy yourselves!"

Nicky put the corner of the treaty into the flame. As it touched, yet another shot rang out. Nicky jerked, staggered, then fell.

From where she lay on the floor, Lydia lowered Olga's derringer, which she had, unnoticed, managed to retrieve. Makarios and Stefano stood in shock, their guns at their sides, too surprised to react.

Nicky looked across the floor at Lydia in amazement. Their eyes met as his world darkened.

Woodford rushed forward to retrieve the treaty as Olga rushed to kneel beside Lydia.

"Thank God," Woodford said, "there's only a corner singed."

"And Lydia," Olga rejoiced, "has only a superficial wound in her arm."

Woodford joined Olga and knelt beside Lydia. He pressed his handkerchief against his daughter's arm. "That was a brave thing you did, my dear. I'm proud of you."

Lydia's eyes were downcast. "You will not be proud when you learn the truth about me."

Olga put her arm around Lydia. "We each have much in our pasts that we regret, Lydia. But who we are at this moment is all that counts. We are a family again. And family is loved, unconditionally."

She and Woodford took Lydia in their arms.

Woodford looked up at Makarios. "You will have them taken for treatment, will you not?"

Makarios said, "I will go with them myself." He signaled three of the waiters, and together they took Lydia and the still unconscious Nicky to the aid station.

With a whimper, Olga collapsed, shaking. The strain of the past half hour was too much, and the ravages of her drug withdrawal returned. Woodford caught her and lifted her in his arms. He turned to face Stefano, who stood guard at the top of the stairs. "I am taking her to my study. Do what you will."

Stefano stepped out of his way and nodded to Gregorio, who assumed control of the hostages as Stefano followed Woodford into the hallway. John moved to follow, but Gregorio blocked his way.

* * *

In the barracks, candles and lanterns lit the cots where the wounded soldiers and Father Demetrius lay. The town doctor had been summoned, and joined by two nuns from the nearby convent, he bent over the still-unconscious priest, closing his wound. He looked up as Makarios and the waiters brought Lydia and Nicky in.

"Put them there," he ordered, indicating the cots next to the three soldiers, none of whose wounds were serious.

"I'm all right," Lydia said, "it's only a flesh wound."

The doctor quickly confirmed that this was so. He turned to one of the nuns. "Clean and bandage this, please, sister." He turned then to work on Nicky, who was now awake and moaning in pain.

As she was being bandaged and her arm wrapped in a sling, Lydia watched the doctor inject Nicky with morphine, then begin probing his wound. "How is he?" she asked.

"The bullet was small in caliber," the doctor answered as he worked, "but it struck him in the chest."

"I couldn't aim that little gun very well. I didn't intend to kill him."

"There is no exit wound, so the bullet is still inside. His survival will depend on removing it, assuming that it has struck no vital organ." The doctor looked up at Sergeant-Major Bledsoe, who was standing beside his wounded men. "He should go to the hospital in town for surgery at once."

"Take him," Bledsoe said to the guards. "But stay with him. He's still a prisoner."

As the guards came forward to lift Nicky, Lydia stopped them and asked Bledsoe, "Can I have a moment with him, please?"

Bledsoe nodded and signaled the guards back. Lydia knelt beside Nicky and whispered to him.

"Nicky, I'm sorry."

Nicky was barely awake. He licked his lips, his mouth dry. Lydia took a glass of water from the bedside and lifted it to his lips. He drank a mouthful, but most ran down his chin. Lydia wiped it gently away and Nicky looked up at her. She was so beautiful in the candlelight.

She whispered again, "I had to stop you."

Nicky nodded slightly. He tried to speak, but Lydia put her finger to his lips and said, "I think I understand why you hit me, and I forgive you. I might have done the same."

Nicky smiled faintly, his eyes glistening.

Lydia came so close he could feel her breath on his cheek. "Tell me where they are. I'll make it right."

She could barely hear Nicky's whispered response. "Vase."

Lydia nodded and touched her lips to Nicky's cheek, then looked up.

Bledsoe nodded to the guards, who carried Nicky out.

Lydia turned to the doctor. "I'd like to go back now."

"Yes, certainly."

Lydia went out into the night.

Makarios leaned over Father Demetrius. The priest was awake, but his eyes were half-closed. "Can he hear me?" Makarios asked the doctor.

"I had to give him morphine when I sutured his wound," the doctor answered, "but I think he is barely awake."

Makarios leaned very close to the priest and spoke into his ear. "Father, you must tell us what to do. We are holding the guests hostage, but the embassy is surrounded by the British soldiers."

Father Demetrius' eyes fluttered. By a sheer act of will, he whispered, though the attempt caused him terrible pain in spite of the morphine. "Make them tell the world that we want only what is ours. Then let them go."

"And what of us and the others?"

Father Demetrius looked into Makarios' eyes and said only, "Amnesty."

* * *

Stefano was standing guard outside the study door as Lydia approached, her wounded arm in a sling. "I want to see my parents," she said.

Stefano well understood the ties of blood and opened the door for her.

As Lydia entered the study, she saw Olga lying on the sofa, trembling uncontrollably, soaked with sweat. Woodford knelt beside her, dabbing her head with a handkerchief that he wet in a bowl of water, whispering reassurances. Lydia leaned over his shoulder. "How is she?"

"It will be a hard fight, but she will beat it," Woodford said. "How is Nicky?"

Lydia shook her head sadly. "They have to operate, but I hope he'll be all right."

"He believed in what he was doing," Woodford said. "That is to his credit, however much his passion led him to a foolish end."

Lydia went to the bookcase, and with her one good arm she took down the precious antique Grecian vase and set it on the desk.

Woodford watched her, puzzled. "What are you doing?"

Reaching deep into the vase, Lydia withdrew the bag of jewels. She carried them to her father. "Here. These are yours."

Woodford took the bag with trembling hands.

"Thank God," he said. "The island is saved."

"That depends on your point of view," Lydia said ruefully. "I'm not sure Nicky would agree."

"Yes," Woodford allowed, "I suppose. But we all have our duty."

The door opened and Makarios and Stefano entered.

Woodford tucked the bag into his pocket and asked quietly, "You have spoken with Father Demetrius?"

Makarios nodded. "We want only two things in exchange for the freedom of your guests. First, that the world be made aware of our demand for *enosis*."

Woodford nodded. "I promise to bring the matter to the attention of His Majesty's Government immediately. I shall do what I can to fairly represent your... point of view."

"Good."

"And the second demand?"

"Amnesty for all Cypriots who participated in tonight's action."

Woodford considered, then nodded. "That is within my power to grant, and I do, on my honor."

"Then we have a bargain."

Woodford turned to Lydia. "Will you look after your mother, please, Lydia?"

"Of course."

Woodford, Makarios, and Stefano went out toward the dining room, closing the door softly behind them.

Lydia dipped the handkerchief in the water, wrung it, and with her one good arm began to dab her mother's face. Olga's eyes fluttered open and as she focused on Lydia's face, she smiled. "Am I in heaven? For you are an angel."

"No, Mother, no angel. Just your daughter."

"That is more than I could wish for or deserve," Olga said, and closed her eyes.

* * *

When Woodford appeared at the top of the dining room stairs, there was a sudden silence. Makarios stepped beside him and raised his shotgun. There was a gasp and the assembled guests shrunk back in horror. John reflexively rushed forward, but Woodford raised a restraining hand.

Makarios broke the gun, ceremoniously handed it to Woodford, then turned to the armed waiters and signaled. One by one, they set down their knives and cleavers.

Woodford turned to the crowd. "Ladies and gentlemen," he said, his voice with its old vibrancy, "this unfortunate episode is over. We are free!"

There was a moment of shocked recognition, then the dining room erupted in a great cheer. Men slapped one another on the back. Women wept with happiness; some even danced in the aisles.

Over the hubbub, Woodford called, "What we need now is a celebratory dish! Makarios! Let us not let your splendid dessert go to waste!"

Makarios bowed. He signaled and the waiters rushed back into the kitchen to prepare.

The clock in the hallway began to chime twelve.

"My God!" Woodford cried. "In all the excitement I had forgotten the time!"

John also rose. "Let me go with you."

"Hurry," Woodford said, and the two of them rushed to the stairs and down the hallway toward the terrace.

As Woodford and John left, the waiters reentered and began moving through the jubilant crowd, offering the Sunset Ice.

As they enjoyed the refreshing dessert, the natural release of the anxieties of the past hours made everyone giddy and talkative. The waiters distributed coffee and cognac for all, and fine cigars for the men and a few daring women. No one noticed that Makarios and Stefano had disappeared during the dessert.

Glace Coucher de Soleil – Sunset Ice

Put one pound of very ripe strawberries in a silver timbale. Sprinkle them with ten ounces of powdered sugar and two ounces of Grand-Marnier; cover and keep this on ice for half an hour. Then rub the strawberries through a sieve, and dilute the purée with an equal quantity of cold sugar syrup and a few dashes of fresh lemon juice. Freeze until set, then combine it with one pint

> *of whipped cream and let set again for half an hour. Put the ice*
> *preparation into pyramid forms in crystal bowls.*
>
> *This ice gets its name from its color, which should be that of*
> *the western sky during a fine sunset.*

* * *

At the entrance to the maze, Sergeant-Major Bledsoe stepped forward as Woodford and John approached. "Orders, sir?" he barked.

"Hold your positions, Sergeant-Major. I have promised amnesty to the natives, and I will insist that my word be kept."

Whatever Bledsoe may have privately thought of this, he kept his discipline. "Yes, sir! I'll tell the lads."

Woodford went on. "And no one is to follow us into the maze – this is a top secret matter."

Bledsoe saluted. "Yes, sir!"

Woodford turned to enter the maze, then had a thought. "And Sergeant," he said, "an Austrian courier may be leaving here in a few minutes. He is in no way to be interfered with. In fact, do all you can to help speed him on his way. Do you understand?"

"Got it, sir!" Though he could make no sense of these strange orders, Bledsoe knew his duty and stood at attention as Woodford and John ran by him and disappeared into the maze.

Led by Woodford, who knew the maze by heart, they quickly rushed through its twists and turns. As they emerged into the clearing at the center, they stopped short. A figure was standing in the shadows behind the bench, beneath the stature of Athena, wearing a full-length leather greatcoat, his face obscured by a slouch hat pulled low over his eyes.

Woodford stepped forward. "I take it you are from Minister Berchtold?"

The courier answered simply, "*Ja.*"

Woodford held out the treaty and took a few steps toward the courier. "Here is the document, a bit the worse for wear, but intact nonetheless."

"*Ja, gut.*" The courier took the treaty, turned and examined it.

Woodford turned back to John and breathed a sigh of relief. "Thank God!"

Behind him, the courier had struck a match and began to burn the treaty, finishing what Nicky had begun.

John saw the flicker of flame. Forgetting his injured shoulder, he sprinted toward the courier. "Good Lord! Stop!"

The courier spun around, a pistol in one hand and the flaming treaty in the other. John barely reached the bench when the courier swung the pistol and struck John across the face. John fell heavily onto the bench and Woodford knelt to catch him, looking up at the courier in disbelief as the treaty was consumed.

"My God, man, what are you doing?"

The courier dropped what was left of the treaty, stepped on it and ground it into ash, then with a flourish pulled off the slouch hat and shook out her long, blond hair.

Calmly, Shirley answered, "Exactly what I came here to do, Governor."

John lifted himself up. "Shirley?"

"Yes, John, your dear, helpless Shirley."

Woodford couldn't believe his eyes. "But the Austrian courier...?"

Shirley gestured toward one of the boxwood hedges, where the figure of a body could be seen lying in the shadows. "I'm afraid he met with the same unfortunate accident that befell Fraulein Burstner."

John was incredulous. "Shirley! I can't believe that the woman I married, that simple little girl from Kansas, could have...."

"No, *don't* believe it, John. We were not in fact married; the ceremony was rigged, as was our meeting at Mr. Carnegie's mansion in Pittsburgh. And I'm not from Kansas, thank God. Now," she said, waving her gun at them, "if you will both stand against the statue, please?"

John and Woodford had no choice but to comply. Shirley took out a length of rope and began to encircle them, back to back, against the body of Athena.

Woodford asked, "And Father Makarios? The shot came from here."

"Yes, I had to disappoint poor Nicky by shooting his priest. Their silly rebellion would have interfered with my plan."

"And what is that, exactly?"

"I had three objectives. The first two were accomplished by a very lucrative deal I made with Makarios and Stefano – who are by now well away from here – to ensure that the black market trade in Cypriot antiquities will continue to flow unabated to Mr. Carnegie's collection at the Met. And as for the cocaine traffic which Vittorio hoped to inherit, it will now have a new customer; the American national drink is now expanding across the world and a huge supply is needed."

She had finished tying them tight and stepped back. She reached into a pocket and withdrew a packet of letters and a fat envelope. "By the way, Governor, I took these letters from the unfortunate Fraulein Burstner. I'll just hang on to them in case you are tempted to report my role in this affair." She held the envelope under John's nose. "And your ten thousand dollars, John, will pay for the lovely sailboat my new partner has always wanted. It will be invaluable in our new business."

Woodford grunted, then asked, "And your third objective?"

"To destroy the treaty, of course."

John, enraged and ashamed, finally spoke. "But why? Whose side are you on?"

Shirley looked at him disdainfully and shook her head. "Like so many others, John, you think the world is run by politicians and their ideologies, and that one must be on one side or the other." She stepped back, putting the letters and the money back inside her coat. "No, gentlemen, I serve no government, have no political agenda. I represent an international consortium of banks and corporations who have recognized that a world war will be the biggest business opportunity in history. They take no side; arms, munitions, and steel can be sold to both sides simultaneously. The larger the conflict, the greater the profits!"

Shirley took out two kerchiefs and gagged each of them. "Sorry for the inconvenience, but I can't have you sounding the alarm after I leave."

She moved toward the edge of the maze, then turned. "I thank you for a most profitable and delicious evening. As Shirley from Kansas would say, 'Gosh, it's been swell!' Say goodnight to everyone for me. I'll give my compliments to the chef myself!"

And with that, she disappeared into the night.

* * *

28 July 1914 – Vienna
The following telegram was sent by Count Leopold von Berchtold at 11:10 am to Serbian Prime Minister M. N. Pashitch:

The Royal Serbian Government not having answered in a satisfactory manner the note of July 23, 1914, presented by the Austro-Hungarian Minister at Belgrade, the Imperial and Royal Government are themselves compelled to see to the safeguarding of their rights and interests, and, with this object, to have recourse to force of arms.

Austria-Hungary consequently considers herself hencefor-ward in a state of war with Serbia.

* * *

3 August 1914 – London
Sir Edward Grey speaks to the English Parliament:

The lamps are going out all over Europe; we shall not see them lit again in our lifetime.

OTHER BOOKS BY ROBERT BENEDETTI

FICTION

The Long Italian Goodbye
(Available at www.robertbenedetti.com)

Looking for Dreamland
(Available through www.Lulu.com/Benedetti)

TEXTBOOKS
Available through Allyn & Bacon

The Actor at Work, 10 ed

The Actor in You, 4 ed

ACTION! Acting for Film and Television

FROM CONCEPT TO SCREEN: An Overview of Film and Television Production

The Director at Work

Creative Postproduction

Join our mailing list at www.robertbenedetti.com,